BASH and the Chocolate Milk Cows

BASH and the Chocolate Milk Cows

story by BURTON W. COLE
illustrations by BUDDY LEWIS

B&H
PUBLISHING GROUP

Nashville, Tennessee

978-1-4336-8530-9

Published by B&H Publishing Group
Nashville, Tennessee

Dewey Decimal Classification: JF
Subject Heading: FARM LIFE—FICTION \ BAPTISM—
FICTION \ THEFT—FICTION

1 2 3 4 5 6 7 8 • 19 18 17 16 15

For Terry, who, despite how I mangled her name, didn't giggle it off as an April Fool's prank when I asked her to marry me. I love you, "Teresa Ann."

Contents

Chapter 1

Roll Out the
Rain Barrel Kayak

Bash squished a blue Play-Doh snake over the last glittering nail point jutting from the plank seat. "Better safe than screechin' 'bout prickly pants." His nose twitched like a rabbit with the sniffles. "'Sides, only thing better-smellin' than Play-Doh is chocolate."

Sebastian "Bash" Hinglehobb, my weirdo third cousin twice removed—but not removed far enough to keep me from getting splished, splashed, splayed, or splotted—stood inside the jagged hole cut through the middle of the rain barrel lying on its side on the creek bank. I stepped back and tripped over a three-hundred-pound hog rooting through the ground.

"Ow!"

"*Snork.*" Gulliver J. McFrederick the Third—Bash's rust-colored, floppy-eared pig with a perpetual smile—grunted. From flat on my back with my legs hooked over a hog's back, it sounded more like a pig giggle.

There is no Gulliver J. McFrederick the First nor Second, nor any other McFredericks, for that matter. Bash can't stand short, sensible names for his farm critters.

"How come you can't just stick with a dog like a normal kid?" I flicked mud off my hands. "Where is your dog anyway?"

"Uncle Jake O'Rusty McGillicuddy Junior doesn't like the creek so much." Bash swung one leg out of the hole in the barrel, dragged the other behind him, and splatted onto the bank. "Besides, I can't ride him."

I slid off Gulliver. "*Skoink, skoink, skoink.*" The flat end of his springy nose bobbed as he sniffed from the top of my T-shirt to the bottoms of my jeans pockets in case I carried any candy bars. I didn't. "*Skoink.*" Gully snuffled off to the water.

Bash slapped the wooden hull. "Told ya we could build our own kayak. Pretty cool, huh, Ray-Ray Sunbeam Beamer?"

"Stop calling me that. It's Raymond. Or Ray." I glurped out of the mud. "Beamer, if you must. And I still don't see why we can't just walk across the stream to the frog-catching rock. We always did before."

"'Cause that's boring. So we're gonna paddle to the rock to catch frogs."

Straw-colored hair swished atop Bash's bobbing head. Or maybe those were straw-colored brains shaking loose. Two hours into spring break on Uncle Rollie and Aunt Tillie's farm in Ohio, and already I waded up to my T-shirt in mud and my cousin's weirdness.

"When you said we'd build a boat, I figured you were teasing for April Fool's Day," I said.

"That's not for two more days. An' the cows are goin' to give chocolate milk for April Fool's Day."

I crossed my arms. "I might be a city kid from Virginia Beach, but I know cows don't give chocolate milk. Not even brown cows."

Bash grinned. "That's why it's going to be the most awesome April Fool's joke ever. An' you're an Ohio boy now."

"But how—"

"You moved to Ohio last year. In the city."

"Not that. How are the cows going to give chocolate milk?"

"Later, Beamer. Today, we're kayak builders." Bash tossed leftover boards into a red wagon with a pile of screwdrivers, string, screws, chisels, nails, and other tools borrowed from Uncle Rollie's workshop. Baling twine wound around the wagon and trailed off into a pig harness. Gulliver had pulled the wagon across the hayfield to the creek. Bash had ridden Gully. I, of course, had walked.

"I wish Uncle Rollie and Aunt Tillie would get you a pony. Then both of us could ride."

I poked at my glasses and studied the sawed, nailed, and gooped-together contraption Bash called a kayak. A couple stones jammed into where it sank into the ground kept it from rolling into the creek.

The barrel started out as one of those wooden slat things held together by iron rings that you see in old-timey pictures of general stores. Aunt Tillie stood two or three of them beneath downspouts outside the farmhouse. When it rained, water rolled off the roof, rivered through the gutters, gushed down the spouts, and filled the barrels. Aunt Tillie used it for her gardens on sunny days.

She kept a couple spare wooden barrels in a tool shed. Well, only one spare now.

"Are you sure we didn't need to ask first? She'll know it wasn't that robber you told me about who's been holding up stores and stuff the last few weeks. She'll know *we* took her barrel."

"Maybe he steals barrels too. We'll find out when we catch him."

I stiffened. "You didn't say anything about chasing any bad guys."

"I just did. We can solve the mystery, Beams. We'll be heroes."

"We'll be dead when he shoots us. I'm not chasing any robber. I don't want him to catch us." I shivered. "I probably don't want your mom to catch us with her rain barrel either."

"Ma won't mind us borrowing some of her stuff."

I cringed. "That's what you always say, but she always does."

Bash chewed on his tongue, a sure sign that he was thinking his deepest thoughts. Like the creek, you could wade across them. "Why would Ma care if we borrowed an old barrel she's not using?"

"Well, we're going to put it into the creek. It'll get wet."

"Beamer, they're rain barrels. They're supposed to get wet. Duh."

I shook my head. "Only on the inside. The outside's supposed to be dry."

"Not in the rain. The barrel gets soaked on both sides."

"You cut a hole in your mom's barrel."

Bash scratched his ear. "You can't have a kayak without a pilot's hole in the middle. A kayak without a pilot's hole for a guy to sit in isn't a kayak. It's a log."

At the water's edge, Gulliver flopped down, stretched out to let the creek roll over his back, and sighed. Or maybe the sigh came from me.

Bash reached through the pilot's hole and pressed on the bench he'd nailed inside to make sure it held. "'Sides, when we're done, we'll yank the seat out and caulk the cutout part back in place with more Play-Doh. It'll be like new." Bash squinted one eye at the hole. "Should I use the red or yellow Play-Doh for that?"

I stared at him. Definitely straw-colored brains shaking loose up there.

Bash gave me a little shove. "Climb aboard, Beamer, and make sure our kayak doesn't sink."

I pushed back. "It was your idea. You sink or swim."

"Can't." The Basher gripped my wrist and dragged me toward the barrel. "One of us has to stay on shore an' watch for goofs. I'm the engineer, so it's my duty to watch."

I dug my heels into the mud, shook my arm free, and glared at Bash. "I think I see the goof." I stomped away from the barrel boat to sit in the grass.

Bash scurried behind me. "You know chief engineers and inventors never get to have any fun. They gotta stand on shore and watch while brave captains get all the fun an' become famous an' stuff."

"Drowning's not fun. It was your idea. You go down with the ship."

Bash slumped. "Bummer, Beamer. I guess you can't be captain then."

"That's right. Wait. What?"

"Captain. If I'm chief engineer and inventor, that makes you the famous captain. Well, not now. Shoulda figured you'd chicken out of the important stuff." Chief Engineer and Inventor Bash shaded his eyes and peered across the fields. "I wonder if Jig's home. He wouldn't be scared to be a hero captain."

I stepped forward. "Wait a second. Hero captain's good, right?"

Bash shoved his hands into his jeans pockets and shrugged. "Yep. And brave and famous. The hero captain runs the ship. He's in charge of everything."

I nodded. "That sounds like me. I turned twelve in February. You're still eleven. So I'm older. Smarter too. That makes me the boss of you."

Bash turned away, probably so I couldn't see how the

truth stung. He shuffled toward the ship. "Yep. You should be the hero captain, not me. But you don't wanna, so—"

I jumped up and pulled Bash out of my way. "So nothing. Stand aside, engineer. The captain's coming through."

Bash bumped me aside and made for the kayak. "That's okay, Beams. I get that you're a fraidy-cat, scaredy-minnow. I'll do it."

I practically tossed him aside. "*I'm* the captain, and that's that."

Bash turned his back to me again and shook a little. I hoped he wasn't crying. "I reckon so." Then he spun, jammed both palms into my back, and shoved. "So hurry up and climb aboard the kayak, Captain, so I can push you into the creek."

While Bash steadied the sideways barrel, I slung one leg through the hole in the side. I pulled my other leg inside the sitting hole and sat on the plank bench. "Is the seat supposed to tilt like this?"

"Sure. When you hit the big waves, it'll feel just like you're level."

"It's a creek, Bash. There are no big waves."

He pointed at the rippling water. "That one looks pretty big."

"For Ohio, maybe."

I stretched my legs to the end of the barrel and kicked something. *Clomp.* "You left the hammer in here." I toed around the end of the barrel feeling for holes. *Clang.* "The nails." *Snap.*

"Yikes!" I shook my foot and peered into the bottom of the barrel. "You set a mousetrap?"

7

Chief Engineer and Inventor Bash grinned. "Yep. Didn't want ship rats aboard."

I pulled the mousetrap off my sneaker and tossed it at Bash. "Trust me, the rat's not on the ship."

"Kayak, Beams." Bash slammed his full weight against the end of the barrel and pushed me into the creek. "Ahoy, matey!"

The barrel bobbled on the creek, which smelled like an odd mix of mud milkshakes, wet weeds, and crisp water.

Bash shouted instructions. "Make sure to paddle for the frog-catching rock. If you miss it, you'll float all the way up Conneaut Creek to Lake Erie. Then you could paddle all the way out to Niagara Falls, an' go over in a barrel kayak."

The current caught the barrel and pulled me toward the middle. "Hey, wait a minute. You didn't tell me that part." I slapped around the inside of the barrel. *Uh-oh.* "Where's the paddle?"

"All right, Beamer. You discovered the goof. You forgot to make a paddle."

I started to yell something about heading up the creek but heard a splash. Then *glub, glub, glub, snorrrrk.* The glubs and gags came from me. Creek water stung my nose and burned down my throat. My head bounced along the pebbles on the bottom of the creek.

I'd discovered the second goof—and maybe my last: barrels roll.

Chapter 2

The Expedition of the Mighty Frog Hunters

A fleet of tiny fish skittered past my upside-down eyes. One darted between my cheek and glasses. Another bumped into my nose. I gurgled. It's hard to hold your breath with a minnow wedged up your nostril.

Four porky legs swished in front of me. A pig snout poked my forehead.

I pumped my legs, pedaling as if I rode a submarine bicycle until I kicked the barrel clear. I flickered like the fish, pushed off the creek bed and burst through the surface. I shivered in waist-deep water and tried to dry my eyeglasses against my soaked T-shirt.

Gulliver J. McFrederick the Third swam a circle around me, *skoinked*, and headed back to shore.

Bash rolled on the bank, collapsed in laughter. "That . . . *snnnrk* . . . that was . . . *heeheek* . . . awesome, Beamer. Do it . . . *mmmgulmp* . . . again."

I spit a stream of creek water at him but missed. "Basher, barrels roll!"

Bash held his sides like his ribs hurt. "Tow it in, Cap'n Beamer, before it gets away. We'll build stabilizers."

"And a paddle. Don't forget the paddle. I know a couple good uses for a paddle."

Chief Engineer and Inventor Bash exploded into another fit of laughter. I splashed ashore, dragging the barrel behind me. Creek water sloshed out of the pilot's hole like a sideways Super Soaker that somebody forgot to cap.

Bash clambered to his feet and grabbed the kayak. "Park it here."

"Dock."

"What?"

"Tractors get parked. Boats get docked." I sploshed to the ground, intending to dock myself against a tree.

Bash kicked at my sneaker, shooting a mini-spray of water over the grass. "Don't park yourself now, Beamer. We gotta go get the stabilizers."

I tried again to dry off my glasses, which only smeared them more. "From where?"

The Basher tipped the red wagon, dumping the tools into

a heap in the grass. He hitched the twine wagon harness over Gulliver, jumped on the hog's back, and waved. "Follow me."

"*Rweeeeet, rweeeeet, rweeeeet.*" Gulliver trotted across the hayfield between the creek and the farmhouse. The empty wagon banged, bounced, and clattered behind them. I sloshed to my feet and followed, my sneakers squishing with every step.

In the dairy barn, Bash yanked boards off a cow pen that wasn't being used. "Pops said he was thinking about takin' it down anyway. We're just helpin'."

Maybe we were. It's hard to think straight with ice-cube blue jeans stuck to your skin and minnow breath up your nose. Bash handed me one of the boards and we ran back to the creek, the boards bumping behind us.

Chief Engineer and Inventor Bash sorted through the pile of tools on the bank until he found a tape measure. He marked lines a little more than halfway up each side of the rain water barrel. "It sinks a bit when you sit in it. We'll build the stabilizers here."

We nailed the shorter, skinnier boards on opposite sides of the barrel, near the ends, like outstretched arms. We pounded the wider, flatter boards into place lengthwise across arms.

Bash wiped the back of his hand across his sweaty brow. "It's a kayak with wings."

It reminded me of one of those outrigger boats, only not as straight. I walked around the barrel and rubbed my chin. "What about the paddle?"

"Oh, yeah. Be right back." Bash darted up the bank and across the hayfield.

I wondered if the frogs would still be there by the time we finished the kayak. I might as well check.

I waded across the cold creek to the sun-warmed frog-catching rock and watched the water roll by. It burbled against the backside of the rock, splitting into two ribbons of water, and joined up again in a foamy *V* past the rock. Without Bash's constant babbling to drown it out, the creek gurgled a happy whisper. Birds chirped and chipmunks chattered in the shadows of the woods along the other bank. A tractor chugged somewhere. I sucked in a delicious breath that smelled like forest moss and creek mud, held it, and blew it out slowly. Out here a guy could forget about nattering cousins and vicious robbers. Awesome.

Stretched out with the hard, rounded edge of the rock pressed into my belly, I dipped fingers into the calm pool in the cave-like recess and tiny ledge at the bottom of the boulder. No frogs, but little black rubbery-looking things flittered between tiny fish. One of the minnows wriggled through my fingers. I loved lying on the frog-catching rock. So quiet. So peaceful. So—

"Hey! What's the big idea?"

So much for calm. Bash was back and babbling at full speed. "Are you crazy? We gotta kayak across. It's the rules. 'Member? Get back here an' help me finish it."

I sighed, slid into the creek, the cold water filling my sneakers and curling my toes, and waded back to shore. Bash sat on the grass duct-taping two snow shovels onto either end of a rake handle. "It's even better than a kayak paddle. I bet the kayak people'll pay me a lot of money for this invention."

"Especially if they need to kayak in a snowstorm."

12

"Very funny. Now get in, Test Pilot Beamer. It's hero time."

"Not yet." I toed through the pile of tools and junk until I found the cans of Play-Doh. No green. I popped the top on the yellow, squished a glob of Play-Doh through my fingers, and started rolling it. Bash tapped his foot. "C'mon, Beamer. We haven't got all day."

"Just a minute." I grabbed another blurp of Play-Doh and sculpted. I always was pretty good in art class, so it only took me a few minutes to shape the barrel body, bent legs, flat feet and googly eyes of a frog. I plopped the yellow croaker onto the front of the barrel like a hood ornament. "Now the Frog Boat is ready."

I climbed into the crooked pilot's seat. "How come there's a rope tied around one of the stabilizers?"

"When you get to the frog-catching rock, I'm going to pull the kayak back. Then it's my turn."

"After you make sure there are no more goofs." I shook the paddle. The orange plastic shovel on the one end held tight. The dented aluminum one on the other end jiggled a bit. "More tape."

Duct tape screeched like ripped rags as Bash rolled another layer around the end of the aluminum shovel handle to the rake handle middle. "Yeah. An' the rope'll make sure you don't float all the way to Niagara Falls."

I shook the paddle again. Solid. "If this thing goes past the frog-catching rock, I'm bailing. Better yet, I'll bail now and you paddle."

Bash flipped the roll of duct tape at the tool pile. "Captain Chicken getting scared again?"

"No. But you built it. You go."

"It's the rules, Beamer. I'm the engineer. I have to watch." Chief Engineer and Inventor Bash slammed into the back of the barrel, launching me into the creek.

The rain barrel kayak spun around in a wavy circle—but it stayed upright.

Bash chased me along the shoreline. "Paddle! Use the paddle."

I dug the orange snow-shovel blade into the gurgling brook. The current caught the big flat square of shovel and tried to knock it from my hand. The barrel kayak tipped and tottered. "Now what?"

"Keep paddling, Beamer."

By swishing the aluminum shovel paddle end, the barrel bobbed right. I dipped the plastic orange paddle end and pulled, and the barrel shanked left. I clawed the water with dented aluminum. The kayak straightened. Then dipped. Water sloshed over the yellow frog hood ornament.

Paddle right. Paddle left. I began to get it. Lift paddle. Pull. Lift. Pull. The nose of the kayak pointed at the frog-catching rock. Lift. Pull. Lift. Pull. The kayak quivered toward the rock. Lift. Pull. Lift. Pull.

"Bash. I'm steering the boat!"

"Don't crash!"

"Huh?"

The frog-catching rocked loomed straight ahead. I discovered another goof—no brakes.

"How do I stop this thing?" The rock seemed to be racing at me, growing bigger, harder and uglier by the creek-tossed second. I scrunched my eyes shut. This was going to hurt.

"Paddle backward," Bash yelled.

Lift. Push orange plastic shovel. Lift. Push dented aluminum shovel. The rain barrel slowed. Circled. Drifted. Circled. *Maybe, just maybe . . .*

A creek current caught the barrel and slammed it forward. *Crunk.* I rammed the frog-catching rock. The back end of the barrel lifted and nearly tossed me out. *Oof.* My belly smashed into the jagged boards from where Bash had sawed the pilot's hole. *Splash.* The bottom smacked the stream. I ripped away from the hole, taking three belly splinters with me. *Thud.* I hit the back side of the hole as the barrel stopped. The kayak stuck to a crevice in the rock.

I groaned. "Bash, I found the brake. It's the rock." I tugged barrel slivers out of my T-shirt. The yellow frog hood ornament plopped onto the rock. I wobbled my way out onto the boulder and reattached it. Next time, I'd walk to the rock. If he thought it was so great, let Bash get banged about. I almost smiled. "Your turn."

Bash tugged at the rope. "Give it a kick, Beamer."

I planted one sneaker on the barrel rim and pushed. My other foot slipped on the wet rock. *Whump.* I landed hard. "Ouch!"

Bash yanked the rope and began reeling the kayak. "Not the way I would have done it, but if it works, use it."

"Stop laughing. It hurts."

"Then don't do it that way." Bash pulled the rain barrel onto the creek bank. He scooped a handful of the junk from the tool pile into the rain barrel—"In case we need to make repairs"—climbed in and used the shovel paddle to push himself into the stream. Bash cut the paddle through the water and powered the kayak straight to the backside of the rock where I stood rubbing my backside. No jostles. No spills. No crashes.

It wasn't fair.

Bash tossed me the rope. "Tie us up, Beamer."

I held the rope end and looked around the rock. "On what?"

Bash scratched his ear. "Hmm. We should have built a pier. Loop the rope around the rock."

I twisted the rope around the boulder three times before the kayak snugged up.

Bash and I dropped to our bellies, hanging over the front of the rock. Something glurped into the water, then two more. Frogs. Widening rings rippled where the frogs dove in from the tiny ledge tucked into the recess of the rock just above the waterline. They disappeared among the minnows and black blobby things. We dangled our arms into the water, twirling around the frog-jump rings.

I sighed. It only took three hours to finally make it out to the frog-catching rock, the rock we could wade to in fifteen seconds. "Bash, you know we could have—"

I nearly jumped clean off the rock when a voice shot out from the shadows of the woods: "Stick 'em up!"

Chapter 3

Frogs and Robbers

I flattened myself against the rock. Bash popped up. I grabbed him and slammed him down.

"Leggo, Beamer." He sat up and waved to the robber in the woods. "C'mon over!"

I grabbed a fistful of Bash's T-shirt and yanked. "Are you nuts? We've got to hide."

Bash shook away. "From Bonkers? Why?"

I peeked past Bash. Bash's neighbor and best buddy—besides me, I mean—Christopher "Bonkers" Dennison strolled out of the trees, a goofy grin almost wiping out his whole face. "Gotcha! April Fool's Day is going to be so easy with you around."

I collapsed. "That's not funny, guys."

Bonkers waded across from his side of the creek in about fifteen seconds. "So when did you get here, Beamer?"

"Mom and Dad dropped me off this morning."

Bonkers winked one brown eye. "Even with the robber hanging around the country? Ooh, pretty brave, city boy."

Bash grinned. "Beamer says we're gonna be detectives and catch him."

"I did not! No detectives. No catching." I peered into the trees. Something moved. Maybe. Where would a robber hide out anyway? In the woods? I stared deep into the trees until my eyes hurt. Maybe not. I blinked. "Um, guys, should we be out here alone?"

Bash flipped onto his back and stretched. "We're kids. It's spring break. We don't even have lunch money."

Bonkers plopped onto the edge of the rock. "The robber only holds up stores. Two weeks ago, it was the feed mill."

Bash nodded. "He cleaned out the cash register. He started to drag away a burlap sack till he figured out it was fulla field corn. So he grabbed three chocolate bars off the counter."

Bonkers brushed some creek gunk off his wet socks. "He held up Lily's Greenhouse last week. Scared Lily with a gun he pulled halfway out of his pocket. He took twenty bucks and some cupcakes she'd baked for lunch."

"Chocolate?" I guessed.

"Yep."

Bash sat up. "Couple days ago, he tried to get the Fertigs'

18

roadside maple syrup stand. Ol' Martha Fertig beaned him with a jug of syrup." Bash thumped the rock. "She soaked him with the whole gallon. Now he can't sneak up on anybody. If ya smell maple syrup, and it's not breakfast, it's the robber."

I aimed my nose toward the woods and sniffed. I smelled creek water, but no maple syrup. "Did he ever shoot anybody?"

"Nope."

"Break into houses?"

Bash laughed. "Nobody breaks into farmhouses. We own pitchforks."

"Mad bulls," Bonkers said.

"Varmint guns," Bash said.

"Barn cats with razor claws."

"Manure piles an' throwin' shovels."

"Mary Jane's got a watchgoat that's crazy goofy. Morton butts anybody who goes near him."

Bash tapped his head and grimaced. "I know. I taught Morton the head-buttin' game when he was a kid. He got real good at it. He's a natural."

"Well, duh, Morton's a goat."

I threw up my hand like a crossing guard. "So who is he? The robber, I mean. Why doesn't anybody stop him?"

Bonkers shrugged. "He just showed up one day and held up Benson's Tractors and Gas. Didn't get anything but chocolate Tootsie Roll Pops from the jar on the counter. He pops up about once a week, steals chocolate, maybe some money, then hides."

Bash nodded. "The sheriff's been running extra patrols, an' Pops and lot of the guys been hanging out at the shops when they can. But it's a big county, an' it's plantin' season, so most of the guys are in the fields all day."

I sniffed again. The thought of pancakes made me drool. "So we're safe?"

Bash rolled over and stared into the water. "Yeah. He won't be back for another five or six days. Unless ol' Mrs. Fertig scared him off for good. Then you'll never get a chance to catch 'im."

"I'm not catching any robbers."

Bonkers stared into the clouds. "Something tells me you will."

I gulped. "You tell something I won't."

Bonkers sighed. "Ah, like Bash said, he won't be back for five or six days."

I let out a gush of air. I might be safe back in the city before the gun guy showed up again. Phew.

Bash wheeled around and sat up so fast that I nearly jumped off the rock. Again. My eyes rolled about a million miles an hour as I tried to spot the robber sneaking up on us with his maple-syruped gun.

Bash pointed at the barrel. "Bonkers, I forgot. Didja see our kayak?"

"Cool." Bonkers slid to the rain barrel. I clutched my chest to keep my heart from jumping out. Bonkers untied the mooring line, and pushed the kayak free from the rock. "Be right back."

I poked at my glasses. "What are you doing? You're already here."

"I didn't paddle over." Bonkers hopped back into the creek and waded to shore, pulling the barrel behind him.

I rolled my eyes. "But you were here."

Bonkers climbed into the pilot's seat and pushed into the creek with the snow shovel paddle. Flashes of orange, then aluminum, shot out of the water and cut back into the stream as he paddled back. "This is awesome, Bash. Now we don't have to wade. We can stay dry."

I grabbed two fistfuls of hair. "But your feet already were wet. Then you splashed through the creek again to paddle back."

The barrel bumped into rock. Bash grabbed the line. "Welcome aboard, Admiral Bonkers."

Bonkers clambered out. "At ease, sailor."

I slapped the rock. "But you already were aboard. You left. And came back. You aren't making any sense."

Bash nodded toward me. "Touch of sea sickness. He's not thinking straight."

"Am too. You clowns are just . . . just . . ." I couldn't think of the word.

Bash nudged Bonkers. "Having fun yet?"

Bonkers winked. "Yep, April Fool's Day is going to be so easy."

"Aargh!" I rolled back onto my belly to search for frogs. I needed intelligent company for a change.

Bonkers dropped down beside me. "See any?"

I glared at Bash. "I see a frog-faced toad."

Bash elbowed me. "I see a toad-faced frog."

Bonkers peered into the water. "I see tadpoles."

"What?" All I saw were minnows and the rubbery black fish.

Bonkers skimmed his finger just above the water surface. "Tadpoles. Pollywogs."

I shrugged. Bonkers sighed. "Baby frogs."

I shook my head. "No, no, no. You knuckleheads aren't pulling that trick on me. Those are fish, not frogs."

Bash chortled into his shoulder. Bonkers scratched his head through his cap. "I'm not joshing you. Tadpoles grow up to be frogs."

Bonkers planned to become a veterinarian. His dad worked for the Ohio Division of Wildlife helping hurt animals. The Dennison place looked like a woodlands zoo. Bonkers knew his critters.

No way. I scooted further over the frog-catching rock. In the calm pool below, hundreds, maybe millions, of little black rubbery blobs with long, swishy tails flittered through the water. "Where are the long legs? The bug eyes? The frog face?"

Bash draggled a tan arm over the rock. "Beamer, you know about caterpillars, right? How they become moths or butterflies?"

"Well, yeah, they spin themselves into cocoons and come out as butterflies. Or better yet, big moths."

Bash nodded. "Yep. Just like Transformers."

Bonkers rubbed his chin. "Or like Bruce Wayne running into the Batcave and roaring out the other side as the Batman in the Batmobile. It's called metamorphosis—changing from one form into another."

I watched the ugly little swishy blobs. "So those things spin cocoons and turn into beautiful frogs?"

"Not cocoons, Beamer. They transform in the water."

Bonkers dipped one brown hand and came up with a palm full of wrigglers. I watched them slide around. They didn't bite Bonkers, so I dunked a pasty palm into the water and scooped up a handful. The squirmy things tickled.

"These guys become frogs? Hey, there are teeny tiny legs on that one. And this one."

Bash scooped his own batch. "Yep." He caressed one wriggly black dot. "See, this one still has tiny gills like a fish. An' this one with the little nubs, those are the back frog legs starting to poke out. It's beginning to transform."

I leaned closer. "They're not growing."

Bonkers slipped his hand into the water and released his pollywogs. "It's not that fast. It takes about three months from the time the momma frog lays the eggs until the eggs pop out tadpoles, and the tadpoles morph into frogs." He trailed a finger through the water, petting pollywogs. "Any with hind legs are about two weeks away from becoming frogs. That one with front leg nubbins is about a week away."

Bash and I released our tadpoles. I left my hand in the water. Darting pollywogs with fluttery tails tickled between my fingers. "Can we take them home and watch?"

Bonkers sat up. "Bash, do you still have that aquarium?"

"Yeah. I keep my socks in it."

Bonkers wrinkled his nose. "You might want to clean it out first. Anyway, fill it about half full with five gallons of creek water. Tadpoles need lots of fresh water, shade, some clean sticks or rocks or stuff out of the water to cling to as their legs grow."

I nodded. "What do they eat?"

"Boil some lettuce or cabbage leaves. Feed them a pinch of leaves every few days. And change the water when it gets dirty."

I watched the pollywogs. "How do we get them to Bash's room?"

Bash jumped up. "I know." He leaned into the rain barrel kayak. I heard tools and junk clunking and splashing around inside the kayak. "With this." He held up an empty peanut butter jar. Bash unscrewed the red lid, clanked around until he came up with a screwdriver, and poked holes in the lid. The plastic lid cracked. "That's okay. It's just for air until we get them home."

I took a big whiff from the peanut butter jar. Ahh. Maybe there is something besides chocolate that smells better than Play-Doh.

I dipped the plastic jar into the creek, letting water and tadpoles gush inside. "I think I got a hundred."

Bonkers squinted at the jar. "Forty or fifty, maybe."

Bash screwed on the lid. "A bunch of 'em have little leg starts."

I sat up and looked across the creek. Dragonflies buzzed the water. Birds flitted about the shore down the way. A cool breeze flicked through my hair. I didn't smell any maple syrup.

Bash took the jar. "C'mon, get in the kayak and paddle it to shore first. Then I'll tow it back."

I looked at the water pooling in the bottom of the rain barrel. Either the Play-Doh wasn't holding or Bash missed a spot. I slid into the stream. "No thanks. I'll walk."

"Me too." Bonkers splashed down beside me. "You want us to tow you?"

"Nope. I'm gonna paddle. Here, take the future frogs so I don't spill 'em."

I took the tadpoles and Bonkers and I sloshed across the creek. Churning the snow shovel oar madly, Bash shot past us. "See ya, slowpokes."

I held the peanut-butter jar up to the sun and watched the little critters dart around. "Do you think we should tell Bash he forgot to untie the kayak?"

Bonkers shook his head. "Nah. He'll find out in about five more seconds."

Twang.

Splash.

"Hey! *Glub.* You guys forgot to untie the rope!"

We watched Bash shake the water from his straw-colored hair while kneeling in the stream. "C'mon, Slowpoke Bonkers, let's get the tadpoles to that aquarium while we wait for the kayak racer."

Bonkers picked up the pail from the pile of tools and filled it with creek water. "Right behind you, Slowpoke Beamer. Right behind you."

Chapter 4

Planning for Pranks

The bloodthirsty roar of a lion ripped through my skull. Through scrunched eyelids, I saw drool roll down gleaming fangs, and drip in deadly droplets on my neck.

Not again.

I yanked the blanket over my head. "Bash, shut off that stupid zoo-animal alarm clock. It's not funny."

Through the muffling protection of the blanket came a sound more frightening than any lion—the wide-awake voice of Bash. "C'mon, Beamer, get up, get up, *get up!* The

Moovarians are attacking the Cluckorians. We gotta stop 'em."

Oh, no. April Fool's Day already? No. This was Tuesday. I was safe until tomorrow. I eased the blanket below my eyes. "What's a Moowhovian?"

"Not Moowhovian. Moovarian. And they're after the Cluckorians. We're gonna blast off and get 'em. Right after breakfast and chores."

I rubbed my eyes. Shook my head. Even pinched myself. Yep, awake. Nope, the showers of Bash-sense raining over my yawning brain still splashed nothing but nonsense. "Bash, can't it wait till morning?"

"It *is* morning. C'mon, Beamer, it'll be epic fun."

I groaned. Yawned. Tossed back the blanket. A swarm of tiny, black spiders littered my pajamas and cascaded across the sheets on either side of me. I sighed. "Bash, that is so lame. I'm the one who gave you that box of plastic spiders for Christmas, remember?"

"Just practicing for tomorrow. Got any ideas?"

I tried to stop the grin. "A couple, maybe. This time, I'm not letting you get all the laughs."

"Cool. Get out of bed an' tell me."

I sat up and swatted plastic spiders to the floor. I slid off the bed into my slippers.

Schplooop!

I flopped backward, shaking goopy slippers onto the floor. "Yuck. What's that?"

Bash snickered. "Shaving cream. Mint. Pretty neat, huh?"

I glared. "C'mere a sec."

Bash stepped closer. I plopped white-splotted feet into his chest, and trailed globs of foam down his shirt, wiggling my toes as I went. "Consider yourself got."

Bash flicked white splashes to the rug and laughed. "Don't worry, Beams. I'm not going to get you anymore. Much. You're too easy. I like a challenge."

"Thanks. I think."

I pulled my glasses from the nightstand and dropped them onto my face. I padded on shaving-creamed feet to the tadpole tank on Bash's desk near the window. Little blobs swirled around the open water at the end of the tank. Others flittered about the ledge we built with sticks, stones, and leaves at the other side. Their tails looked shorter. "Any frogs yet?"

Bash shook a couple bits of lettuce into the aquarium. "Not yet, but look at that guy. I think the front legs are popping out."

I leaned so close that my nose touched the glass. "Yes, I see him. That one too. These little goobers are growing legs. Awesome."

Bash grabbed my pajama collar and yanked. "Now c'mon, before Ma yells at us to hurry up. What's your lame-o idea for April Fool's Day?"

I rooted through my backpack for a clean T-shirt. "Why do you want to know?"

"Why do you want to pull a prank? You don't do pranks."

"You guys keep saying I don't know how to have fun. Well, I do."

Bash scratched his ear. "Dunno, cuz. You might want to leave pranks to the pros."

"So how come you want to know my plans? Are you scared of my brilliance?"

"Ha. No way. It's just that . . ." Bash sighed. "I've figured out everything except how to get Mary Jane's goat."

I rubbed my shoulder. Bash's pesky neighbor Mary Jane was older, taller, and scarier than any of us. "Why get Mary Jane? She'll just clobber us again."

"Not Mary Jane. Her goat. Ol' Morton, the white goat she shows for 4-H at the county fair. We're gonna hide him or teach him to play baseball or something. I haven't decided. Morton's cool."

"Does Mary Jane still wear the pointy-toed cowboy boots?" My shins twitched.

"Only to church an' school. Unless she's after me. Then anywhere. So c'mon, what were you gonna do?"

I tilted my open backpack toward Bash. "The only goat I meant to get was you."

The Basher peered into the backpack. His eyes widened. "Awesomeness, Beamer."

He took the backpack, reached inside, and pulled out the spray cans of temporary hair coloring—glowing gross green, nasty blazing orange, shiny putrid purple, and a hurt-your-eyes bright blue. "When?"

"Tonight. While you slept." I shrugged. I never could keep a secret. "Guess I can't now."

Bash tested a squirt of purple on his fingertip. "Why not? It'd be hilarious. It'll freak out Ma."

"And the cows, pigs, and chickens." I picked up my sneakers. "Bash, you can't prank someone if they know it's coming."

"Morton doesn't know."

My sneakers clumped to the floor. "No. Oh, no. No, no, no! You're not coloring Morton. Tell me you're not going to spray-paint Mary Jane's goat."

"Why not? It'll wash right out. It'll be the best trick I've ever pulled on Mary Jane."

"And probably the last." I grabbed the hair coloring cans out of Bash's hands, stuffed them into my backpack, zipped it, and shoved the backpack under the covers. *"No."*

Before Bash could answer, Aunt Tillie's voice boomed up the stairs. "Boys! If you don't get down here now, you'll be doing chores without any breakfast."

Bash's eyes darted to the alarm clock. "Oops. We're late. C'mon, we gotta get chores done so we can fly our space shuttle to Cluckoria." He dashed from the room.

Why can't cows eat breakfast at eleven o'clock instead of six? I dropped to the bed. A plastic spider dug into my leg. I flicked it to the floor and stared at my shaving cream-covered slippers. What if we gave Morton the beauty parlor treatment? Mary Jane would drag us into her parlor and work some beauty all over us, that's what. I was too young to be beauty-parlored.

I tugged on the rest of my barn clothes. "You guys got any tips for me on that Transformers stuff?" I asked the darting and swirling tadpoles. I swirled my finger around the polly-wogs. A brush of teeny tiny frog foot-in-the-making tickled my fingertip. "You guys get to turn into frogs. I'll be stuck as the cousin of the guy who got Mary Jane's goat."

An hour or so later, we climbed back over the fence around the pig pasture after cleaning the hutches and filling the feeder. Bash dropped to the ground and crumpled his green baseball cap back into place. "I'll gather the eggs from the chicken coop, and you clean behind the cows."

I jumped, stumbled, and squished one knee into spongy spring grass. "Not fair. There are a lot more cows than chicken eggs."

"Yeah, but I gotta feed and clean the chickens too. You only gotta clean the milking barn. The cows stay inside only long enough to be milked."

"And to plop some some pretty big messes. Bash, I have to use a shovel and a wheelbarrow."

"Better'n using your hands."

A reddish blur flashed from behind an orange tractor parked in the yard. I pivoted to the side and threw up an arm and a leg to protect myself. That left me off balance when, in cascades of barking, Bash's Irish setter Uncle Jake O'Rusty McGillicuddy Junior crashed into me, toppling us both to the ground. After a few moments of the slobberiest tongue lashing I ever had, I wrestled the dog away in a fit of giggles. Dog tongues tickle.

"I'm happy to see you too, Uncle Jake." Tussling his red head, I tottered back to my feet. Uncle Jake bounded around my legs. I plucked off my glasses and wiped away dog slobber with my T-shirt. "He's even more excited today than when I showed up yesterday."

Bash winked. "Yesterday, you didn't have sausage gravy splots on your T-shirt."

I must have been shoveling Aunt Tillie's biscuits and gravy so fast that some of it escaped. I pulled up my T-shirt and sucked the sausage spots that Uncle Jake missed. Yeah, Aunt Tillie's sausage gravy and biscuits are that good.

Bash stepped away. "Have fun with the cows, Beams. I'm flyin' to the coop."

It was when I turned to grab Bash by the collar that I saw a girl running way down the road. I recognized the way her black hair bounced. "Bash. It's Lauren. *She's running.* Is it the robber? Is he chasing her? You guys said the robber with the gun wouldn't be back yet."

Bash waved. "No robber. Lauren runs all the time now. For fun."

"Nobody runs for fun."

Lauren Rodriguez waved back. Then she locked eyes on me. I heard a squeal, and she kicked it into high gear. Uh, oh. I searched for a place to hide.

"Raymond, you're back!" Lauren blasted into the driveway. I pivoted to the side and threw up an arm and a leg to protect myself. That left me off balance when, in cascades of hellos, Lauren caught me in a great big sweat-soaked hug.

"No hugging! You're a girl. And you're drowning me."

Lauren let go and hit me with a giant dental-exam grin. "It's so cool that you're back."

I flapped my T-shirt to dry out the sweat splotches. "Why are you running if the robber's not chasing you?"

Lauren's teddy bear brown eyes sparkled as she sucked in great gobs of air. "I joined track. I run the 800, the 1600, and the hurdles. Spring break is no excuse to break training. What happened to your shirt?"

"Dog slobber."

Bash smirked. "Sausage gravy."

I glared. He didn't have to tell *everything*. "Now there's girl sweat."

Lauren giggled. And huffed and puffed some more. She turned to Bash. "Hey Pig Boy, are we still rescuing the Cluckorians today?"

She'd been calling Bash Pig Boy ever since we rescued her from a snowbank last winter on an ambulance sled powered by Bash's riding pig, Gulliver J. McFrederick the Third.

Bash threw a thumbs-up. "Yepper. Then we're gonna be detectives, track down clues, and catch the robber."

I jumped. "No robbers. No clues. No guns. No, no, no."

Lauren grinned at Bash. "Excellent. We'll teach those Moovarians and the robber a thing or two." She spun back at me. "Raymond, I'm so happy to see you." I ducked before she could hug me again. "Later, 'gator. Gotta run." She turned on her toes and tore down the driveway. Flapping black hair waved good-bye.

"No detectives. No robbers." I scratched my neck as I watched her go. "That was weird."

"Lauren an' Tyler and their ma moved out of the hunting shack they lived in after comin' up from Florida. They have their own place now. Mrs. R. got a job in town doing counting."

"Accounting?"

"Whatever. Lauren and Tyler come over most every day." Tyler is Lauren's baby—I mean, little brother.

"And you wrestle Moowhatians?"

"Not Moowhatians. Moovarians. Not every day. Sometimes we ride bikes, race go-carts, or chase rabbits in the woods." Bash winked. "Lauren asks about you a lot."

"She does not."

"Does too. Have fun with the cows. Then we're gonna board the Space Shuttle Sebastian and blast off." And Bash blasted off.

I kicked at a stone. Shaving-creamed slippers, painted goats, space shuttles, Moowhyagains, a robber with a gun on the loose, and girl sweat. And it wasn't even April Fool's Day yet.

I turned to the barn. And a big, flat shovel, a wheelbarrow, and whatever's found at the back end of cows. I meant to show the kids that I'd learned how to have fun. I wondered when the fun would begin.

I sighed and trudged toward the milk barn. And stopped. What in the world was a Moovarian, anyway?

Chapter 5

The Chicken Shuttle Space Coop

I scratched a circle with my sneaker toe in the upper right corner of a tic-tac-toe pattern etched into the gravel driveway. "Got you this time."

"Nope." Bash toed an *X* in the opposite corner and dug a line through three *X*'s down the left side. "That's seven in a row for me. Still none for you."

I smeared the board with my shoe. Chunks of stone bumped under the bottoms of my rubber soles. "So chores are done, and it's still a couple hours until lunch."

"Dinner. We call our food breakfast, dinner, and supper. And dessert."

"Lunch, dinner, whatever. What are we waiting for?"

"That." An egg-yolk yellow car pulled into the driveway, gravel crunching and popping beneath its tires. Uncle Jake blasted toward the car, skidding to a stop at one of the back doors, his bushy red tail swishing so fast that it looked like he meant to start a dust storm. Bash whooped. "It's space shuttle time."

A back door of the yolk cracked open, and a tan kid not much bigger than a chick flapped to the ground and scratched to get his footing. "Let's play, let's play!" peeped Tyler Rodriguez, Lauren's four-year-old brother. Uncle Jake barreled into him, and the two tumbled into a slobbery, giggling, barking mess.

Lauren slid out of the front passenger side of her mom's car and smoothed her shirt. She did that head toss thing girls do, whipping a long length of raven hair over her shoulder. I backed up in case she tried that huggy stuff again.

"Hey, Raymond. Still wearing gravy stains, I see."

I clamped my hands over the spots. "Um, hey."

Lauren spun toward Bash. "So, Pig Boy, are we set for tomorrow morning?"

Glittering blue eyes narrowed over Bash's grin. "Yepper."

"What?" I asked.

Bash shook his head. "Not yet. You'll blab."

"Will not."

"It's a surprise. You're part of it. But now"—Bash grabbed Tyler's collar and separated boy from dog—"we've got some rescuing to do. C'mon, Super Ty, let's get aboard the Space Shuttle Sebastian." They took off on a run.

I tried to smooth the chewed gravy part of my T-shirt. "What's tomorrow? What space shuttle?"

Lauren giggled. "Tomorrow's April Fool's Day. And Tyler and Pig Boy pretend the chicken coop is a space shuttle and fly off to have all kinds of crazy adventures."

"And you let them?"

She winked. "Sometimes it's fun pretending to be a little kid."

I studied the chicken coop. It was new, built since I last visited the farm. It stretched out a long way, and probably could hold a hundred chickens even though Aunt Tillie hardly ever kept more than three dozen. White with black trim, the coop did resemble a space shuttle, minus the wings. Shuttle wings, I mean. It had plenty of chicken wings.

Lauren punched my shoulder. "So, let's go." Like Bash and Tyler, she ran past the chicken coop door and rounded the corner. I trudged around the side to find Lauren crawling up a little ladder plank leading up to one of the chicken-sized pop-up doors at the bottom of the wall. "Through here." She shot through the pop door like a missile in rocket sneakers.

I dropped to my knees and started squeezing through the hole. My heart pounded when I got jammed halfway through. Maybe I should have skipped that last round of biscuits and gravy. Bash and Lauren each grabbed an arm and yanked.

"*Ow.* Hey, the arms don't come off. Stop yanking."

Bash tightened his grip. "Inhale, Beamer."

There should have been a popping sound when they popped me through the pop door. Instead, I plopped face-first onto corn dust and straw scatterings. A large chocolate-brown chicken named Sadie Sue Cackledoo pecked the back of my hand. She marched up my head and down my back, all four toes curling into me with each step, on her way out the little door to strut around the yard.

"Welcome aboard, Beamer," Bash said, bits of straw hiding in his hair. "I'm the admiral, this is Captain Tyler the Great, and we're on a dangerous mission of mercy."

I blew a reddish-brown feather off my lips and wiped something—I didn't want to know what—off my right hand onto a pants leg. "What we're on is the chicken coop floor, and I think it's full of germs."

Admiral Bash shook his head. "Nope. When you walk through the people doors, it's just a chicken coop. When you dive through the secret portals, you're teleported aboard the Space Shuttle Sebastian. There are the control panels." He pointed at chalk scribblings on feed boxes below windows at the other end of the coop.

Tyler danced around Bash, stirring up straw and feathers as he warbled, "We gotta spaceship. We gotta spaceship." He and Bash ran to the other end, plucked pieces of colored chalk from a sideboard, and scrawled in a few more controls on the panels.

I sneezed. The place smelled of chicken dust, powdered corn, and something not quite sweet and not quite what I wanted to think about. I stood, wiped my runny nose on one T-shirt sleeve, my foggy glasses on the other sleeve.

Lauren leaned against a wall, cuddling a black-and-white speckled hen named Cheryl Checkers P. Featherchecker.

I leaned beside her. "Aren't we a little old to be playing spaceship?"

Lauren kissed the top of Cheryl Checkers' feathered head and grinned. "Of course we're too old. We're eleven."

"I'm twelve. My birthday was in February."

"Oh, yeah, you're way too old to play pretend rockets." Lauren rubbed her chin. "Now let's see, what do they call it when a kid who's twelve holds a controller and flies pretend spaceships into pretend space to conquer pretend asteroids and aliens? Oh yeah, *playing video games*. Yep, you're way too old to play pretend with us, Twelvie."

She slid a finger down the point of Cheryl's beak, set the chicken on the floor, spun, and ran for the far end of the coop. "Got anymore chalk? I'll draw new scanner screens."

A brown chipmunk-cheeked chicken pecked at my shoe-lace. I sighed. "Hello, Mrs. Finley Q. Ruffeather Beakbokbok. You think I'm fun, don't you?"

Mrs. Beakbokbok tilted her head as if deep in thought. I squatted beside her. "I suppose Tyler is acting *his* age. But Bash and Lauren, what's up with that?" I petted the leathery red comb on her head. "Oh, sure, they're laughing and having a blast. Well, I can be silly too. I'm not that boring. Am I?"

Mrs. Beakbokbok bobbed her head. I nodded back. "See, I knew you'd understa . . ." I stopped. "Yipes. I'm spilling my guts to a chicken."

Mrs. Beakbokbok pecked my toes. Her sharp beak stabbed right through my sneakers. "*Ow.* Cut it out." She flutter-flapped to the roosting rods, leaving me squatting by myself, rubbing my toes. Well, if I'm goofy enough to talk to chickens, I might as well help chicken-scratch pictures on the coop wall. I stood, brushed chicken dust off my clothes, and shuffled toward the kids. "Got another piece of chalk?"

"All right, Lieutenant Beamer the Chicken-Hearted." Shuttle Admiral Bash clapped chalk dust from his hands. "Attention, people."

We pocketed our chalk and gathered in. A hen strutted around our feet, pecking at pieces of corn and untied shoelaces. Tyler jumped as Bash circled us, flailing his arms as he babbled.

"The planet Cluckorian cracked like an egg when the creatures of Moovaria tripped while jumping over the moon. Now our faithful friends the Cluckorians have no planet and are under attack by the Moovarians. Our mission is to guide this ship through the swarms of Moovarian fighters and relocate the Cluckorians to the planet of Henbeakia in the Red Rooster Galaxy."

I raised my hand. The admiral stopped. "Yes, Lieutenant Chicken-Heart?"

"Stop calling me that." I poked slipping glasses back up the bridge of my nose. "What are Cluckorians, anyway?"

Bash nodded at my foot. "That's a Cluckorian, ripping a hole in your sneaker right now."

"Hey, quit it." I hopped away from Mrs. Beakbokbok.

Tyler ran to one of the coop windows overlooking the cow pasture. "An' see out there in space? Those are Moov'rins."

Uncle Rollie's herd of huge milk cows grazed in the pasture, tails flicking at flies. I finally got it. "Oh. Chickens.

Cluckorians. Because they cluck. And the cows are Moovarians because they moo."

Lauren giggled. "Nothing gets by you, does it, Ray? Probably because you're twelve."

Heat stung my cheeks. "Yeah, well, there aren't a lot of chickens in my Super Galaxy Galactic Black Hole Space Attack video games."

I looked around the chicken coop. A couple rows of straw-stuffed nesting boxes ran along one of the long walls, with another double-sided row of them right down the middle of the narrow coop. Against the other wall at the far end was a network of rods, the roosts on which chickens would flatten themselves out in feathery splotches to sleep. At the near end were pens surrounded by—what else—chicken wire, a place where chicks could be separated out, feed stored . . . or kind of like the space where backup rocket fuel cells are encased in my Super Space Commander of the Planets video game. Or like where the photon torpedoes made ready to launch in my Alien Warthogs Wars game. Yeah, maybe . . .

Bash ran to the storage pen. He came back with an empty watering pail, which he overturned about five feet behind the two windows. He plunked himself atop the pail like a king on his throne. "Attention on the bridge."

I poked at my glasses. "What bridge? I see a bucket. You're on it."

"The bridge is what the ship control center is called." He saluted Lauren. "Commander Navigator Lauren, chart us a course to the Milky Way."

Lauren returned the salute. "Aye-aye, Admiral Pig Boy." She spun on her toe, dashed to one of the nesting boxes, and jabbed into a clump of straw for an old toy cash register. Lauren clicked at the buttons. The register burped a silly *brrrrrrring*. She turned. "Course programmed, Pig Sir."

As special effects go, the chicken shuttle space coop navigational system sure didn't match any video game.

Shuttle Admiral Bash nodded to Tyler and me. "Captain. Lieutenant. Take us out of here."

I looked around. "Huh?"

Tyler tugged at my sleeve. "C'mon, Uncle Beamer. You get that one." He pointed at the feed bin beneath the window on the right. Tyler ran to the bin on the left, and stood on tiptoes to peer out the window. "Ready."

I walked to the other bin. Bash bellowed commands. "Captain, fire the port engines."

"Aye-aye." Tyler stabbed an assortment of chalked buttons.

"Lieutenant, fire the engines on the starboard side of the ship."

"Aye-aye, Admiral." I poked at red, blue and yellow buttons.

Tyler shrieked. *"No!"*

"Wha . . . what?" I jumped back, expecting a crazed chicken or gun-toting robber to jump out and grab me.

"Not those buttons. You crashed the ship!"

Lauren winked. "I don't know how kids get to be twelve without knowing green means go."

"It could have been red. Green kryptonite stopped Superman."

Shuttle Admiral Bash leaped from his bucket. "Commander Navigator Lauren, take over the starboard panel."

Lauren made such a big deal about poking the green

button that chalk dust poofed around her finger. She peered at a screen drawn in chalk between the two windows. "Space shuttle stabilized, Admiral."

"Good work, Commander." Bash saluted Tyler. "Excellent job, Captain Tyler-the-Great. You saved the ship from Lieutenant Beamer the Chicken-Hearted's goof."

"It's a chicken coop," I sputtered.

Tyler patted my arm. "Don't worry 'bout it, Uncle Beam. I'll help you."

Cracked eggs. All of them. Nothing but cracked eggs.

Admiral Bash furrowed his eyebrows. He squinted at the chalk-drawn view screen. "Crew, get ready for hyperdrive. On my mark. Three . . . two . . . one . . . GO!"

Lauren poked a blue dot, pulled at a purple knob and leaned back as if propelled by thruster force. Tyler spun two white knobs and leaned back. Both of them grinned like maniacs as they stared out the windows at the stars they were overtaking at a zillion miles per hour.

It looked a bit like fun.

I closed my eyes. I felt the G's. Maybe I could do this. I scrunched my eyelids harder. Planets whipped by. Yeah, okay, not bad.

I opened my eyes, not to a chicken coop, but to a space shuttle. Awesome. Who says I don't have imagination?

"So what's next?"

Lauren's teddy-bear-brown eyes sparkled. "Why, we're going to egg the cows, of course."

Chapter 6

The Attack of the Moovarians

Lauren spun toward the window. "Admiral! Starboard viewing screen. A herd of the Moovarian fighters approaching."

Bash scrambled to the top of his bridge bucket and cupped his hands to his mouth. *"Woot, woot, woot, woot."*

Tyler patted my hand. "It's okay, Uncle Beam. It's the attack warning." He jumped away like a tiny pogo stick, getting a glimpse out the pasture window with each bound. "I see them. I see them!"

Uncle Rollie's herd of milk cows grazed in the pasture just beyond the windows.

Starship Admiral Bash keyed an imaginary microphone. "Battle stations."

Tyler saluted and scrambled to the top of the feed box on the left. Lauren zipped to the window on the right. I stepped left, then right, then stopped and shrugged. "Where do I go?"

Lauren yanked my T-shirt. "Take this watch. I'll load the photon torpedoes."

"We have photon torpedoes?"

Admiral Bash keyed his make-believe mic. "Prepare the hatches."

Tyler slid his window up. "Prepare hatch, 'Tenant Beam."

I raised my window and drank in a gust of spring air. The herd of Moovarians blasted through space, darting in at us for the . . . plodding in for the . . . daydreaming in . . .

A black-and-white Moovarian ambled three steps in our direction, noticed a thistle, and munched. I turned from the window. "Uh, Admiral, the Moovarians aren't moving."

"Don't let them fake you out, Lieutenant. It's a sneak attack." Bash jumped from his bridge chair and ran to the unused nesting box next to the toy cash register navigational system. He dug a coffee can from beneath the straw and popped the lid. Grain—sort of like chocolate cake for cows.

Bash ran to the window, waved a fistful of the cattle feed, and called out in a sing-song voice, "Come boss, come boss, come boss, come bossy!"

I arched my eyebrows.

"An old spaceman chant," he said. "It was used decades ago to call Moovarians in from star pastures."

"Oh."

Tyler, Lauren, and I scooped grain into our hands and chanted at the grazing cows. One Moovarian, then another, and finally a few more wandered over and slurped from our hands with their big, rough, slimy, supersized tongues.

"Yes. They attack!" Admiral Bash layered another fistful of grain across a windowsill to make sure the attack continued. With the Moovarians finally on the move, we could get back to the business of rescuing the Cluckorians.

"Here." Lauren slapped a big, brown egg with a couple strands of straw stuck to it into my hand. "Cluckorian photon torpedoes!"

Bash took another egg, this one white, and smashed it between his palms. Clear and yellow goo oozed between his fingers and down the nose of an invading Moovarian. She slurped with her big, powerful Moovarian tongue.

Tyler ran at another cow, squishing an egg against the rock-hard bridge of its nose. "Awesome!"

I bounced the egg in my hand. Well, with three dozen chickens each laying an egg a day, Aunt Tillie had more than she could use. And if Bash said it was okay . . . I crunched the Cluckorian torpedo in my fist and rubbed it over the snout of the Moovarian fighter ship poking through my window. Slimy egg goop mixed with cow snot squished between my fingers. "Yuck!"

The cow licked my hand before swiping her own nose. Before I could wipe the cow spit and egg slime on my jeans, Lauren splatted another egg bomb into my palm. "You don't get to do that playing video games, do you, Twelvie?"

We swarmed every roost in the chicken coop for more Cluckorian ammo. Invaders took turns poking their heads in the window for licks of egg-gooped grain.

The eggs ran out. Chicken Shuttle Space Coop Admiral Bash keyed his invisible mic. "Commander Navigator Lauren. Prepare the dairy cannons."

"Aye-aye, Sir." Lauren dashed to another empty nesting box and hauled out four cans of whipped cream. She tossed a can at each of us. We shook them. "Locked and loaded, sir."

We triggered the nozzles over the muzzles of the cows. They lapped up the whipped cream with big swipes of their long tongues and bawled for more. *"Mmmwwwwaaaaaa."*

Tyler swirled plops of whipped cream across big, wet cow noses. "We got 'em. We got 'em."

When Tyler's cream can *phffted* out, Bash handed him his. "It's a secret dairy cannon ammo formula that saps Moovarian powers. Good work, Captain Ty. No longer will they be able to shoot lasers from their eyes."

"We win. We win!" Tyler shot the rest of the whipped cream into his own mouth. He wouldn't be shooting lasers from his eyes for at least two months.

Our ammo spent, the Admiral settled onto his water bucket com chair and keyed his mic. "Lower the shields. Divert all power to the thrusters. We're clear for Henbeakia. The Cluckorians are rescued."

I scanned the chicken coop. Empty except for us rescuers. "I think all the Cluckorians abandoned ship." I tugged off my glasses and tried to find a clean spot on my T-shirt so I could wipe the lenses.

Lauren rubbed her chin, winked, and turned to Bash.

"Excuse me, Admiral Pig Boy, but what if the Moovarians beamed aboard the ship? Then we'd have to rescue the Cluckorians all over again."

Bash scratched his ear. "I hadn't thought about that." He jumped from his water bucket. "C'mon, guys. Let's bring some cows, I mean Moovarians, into the chicken coop so we can kick them out and save the Cluckorians."

"Yay." Tyler ran through one of the chicken pop doors. Lauren zipped out right behind him. I grabbed Bash by his collar.

"There are no Cluckorians left to rescue. They all waddled outside to eat."

"Strutted. Ducks waddle. Chickens strut."

"Whatever. They're gone."

"Which means they need to be rescued. C'mon."

I traced the edges of the pop door with my foot. "How's a cow going to squeeze through there?"

"Um . . . Oh, I forgot to tell you. If Moovarians use the people door, it teleports them onto the ship, 'cause they're not people. That's their secret door."

That made as much sense as anything did today. I gave up.

We were leading a half-dozen Moovarian warriors toward the chicken coop when Aunt Tillie stepped onto the back porch. "Kids, get ready to go to the . . . Where are you going with those cows? Are those egg shells in their hair? And yolk? And butter?"

Bash dipped his finger into a white swirl on a cow's nose and licked it. "Whipped cream."

"Whipped . . . whipped . . ." Aunt Tillie squeezed her eyes shut and took a breath. Quietly, very quietly, she said,

"Sebastian Nicholas Hinglehobb, put those cows away. And then, and then . . ."

We hustled them back to the pasture before Aunt Tillie figured out how to finish her sentence. Bash patted a big, blocky, black-and-white Moovarian on its long, flat neck. "We'll bring you more eggs next chance we get."

Aunt Tillie stood hands on hips, one eyelid flapping, when we rounded the barn again. "Look, you hooligans, wash your hands, and load these pies I baked for the hoagie fund-raiser at the fire hall. We'll go when I finish getting Darla dressed."

She staggered back inside, muttering something we couldn't quite make out.

Bash popped open the trunk of the car. I was placing a strawberry-rhubarb pie inside when Bash grabbed my arm. "I've got a great idea. I know how we're gonna rocket the Cluckorians to the Red Rooster Galaxy."

I froze. Lauren slid an apple pie into the trunk. "How?"

Bash told us.

Lauren whooped. "That will be super excellent."

My pie clumped into the trunk. "No way."

"Beamer, it'll be an awesome warm-up for April Fool's Day tomorrow."

I shook my head. "We're so grounded."

"Nah." Bash's blue eyes glittered. "Fire Chief Willie Hall likes gags."

"He won't like this one."

Lauren punched my shoulder. "C'mon, Raymond, let's go get some chickens."

Tyler darted to the coop. Bash and Lauren ran behind. What could I do?

It took some doing rescuing three dozen chickens who didn't want to be rescued.

Lauren closed the trunk lid and brushed feathers off her shirt. "Phew."

I wiped nose and glasses on opposite sleeves again. "I think one of the red hens sat in the banana cream pie."

Bash pulled off his cap and plucked feathers from it. "It's a big trunk, with air holes. There's lotsa room for pie and chickens. We better turn on the radio so Ma doesn't hear the Cluckorians. We want it to be a surprise."

I popped my glasses back on. "Are you sure?"

"Ma will wonder why she didn't think of this April Fool's trick herself."

"Because it's still March, maybe?"

The chickens stayed mostly quiet. At one bump in the road, a cackling exploded behind us. Bash cooed to three-year-old Darla, "Sissy, what noise does a chicken make? *Bock-bock-bock-baaaawk.* You try it. Louder!" He signaled for us to join in. Tyler made a pretty good chicken. *"BWWWAAAAAAWWWWK."*

Aunt Tillie could cover only one ear at a time. "Will you kids stop that clucking!"

By this time, we were pulling up to the fire hall, which was only about a mile away. The parking lot was full. The twins Jig and Jag were there, snickering with Mary Jane as they munched on brownies. Bonkers and his family headed back to their truck with an armload of sub sandwiches and a cake. Volunteer firefighters showed off shiny fire trucks to a cluster of kids. Grown-ups chattered about whatever grown-ups chatter about: ". . . so Henry said he'd sit up all night with the garden hose across his lap, and when that nasty robber shows up, he's going to show him how hard a firefighter sprays water . . ."

At least, that's what *was* happening.

Then Aunt Tillie popped open the trunk.

Afterward . . . well, my memory's still a little jumbled from the sudden flurry of feathers dripping in strawberry-rhubarb, banana cream, and lemon meringue pie filling.

"Mom, the chicken pot pie got loose!" one girl hollered.

"Aren't you supposed to fry them first?" a laughing guy bellowed. Then a hen pecked at his toe and he howled. It chased him all the way to his pickup, splattering globs of banana cream all the way.

Three little girls jumped into the back of the rescue squad. Two speckled hens flapped in behind them. The girls tumbled out the other side and closed the ambulance doors, leaving the rescued Cluckorians fluttering around stretchers and air hoses.

A chicken flapped-flew just off the ground through the open bay doors of the fire hall, scattering lunch and lunchers, whapping some of each with strawberry-rhubarb pie pieces.

"Cool!" Jig yelled, his arms flapping as he chased a hen toward his sister.

Admiral Bash ran among flying food, bug-eyed people, and pie-dripping chickens, cackling, "April Fool! April Fool!"

Then he noticed Aunt Tillie, who looked like a dancing rope with eight arms and seventeen legs as she ducked, darted, and snatched at hens raining feathers in browns, whites, and speckles.

Bash scratched his ear. "Beamer, I don't think Ma is enjoying our surprise."

"Our?" I spluttered. "That one was all *your* idea, buster."

Lauren skidded to a stop in front of us, a chicken stuffed under each arm. "We may have carried the Cluckorians game too far." She dashed away.

I made a grab for a speckled hen and missed. "Don't just stand there, genius. Round up the chickens."

Two hours later, we headed home with most of the chickens we came with. Chickens flapped, fluttered, squawked, and cackled in Aunt Tillie's car as we roared home without any hoagies for dinner. Or supper.

Chief Willie—who actually did find it funny—promised, "I'll bring back the other two hens when they come out of hiding, or after we have enough eggs for breakfast." He was still laughing when he said, "I'll see you kids later when you come back to wash the fire trucks. All of them."

That wasn't funny.

Bash lifted a wing from his face. "And tomorrow's April Fool's Day. What trick do you wanna do first?"

"Live." I pulled a chicken's toe out of my ear. "I just want to live."

Bash hooted. "Yeah, being alive makes every day great. Oh, hey, we gotta paint Mary Jane's goat."

Great day.

Chapter 7

Run for Your Life or Punishment

I squirmed on the big rock marking the edge of the drive-way. No wonder cavemen look all hunched over in those pictures. Anyone who uses rocks for easy chairs must have rocks in his head. I slid around and grunted like a caveman. "Why are we doing this again?"

"Because you'll love it." Lauren the stork balanced on one leg. She bent the knee of her other leg, tucked her foot behind her, reached around, and pulled at the toe of her shoe until her heel pressed into her backside.

I cringed. "What are you doing?"

"Stretching. Always stretch before you run."

"If I stretched first, I'd never get away from Bash's disasters in time."

Lauren giggled. "You ran a lot at the fire hall today. How many chickens did you catch?"

"One. And two caught me."

"They were teasing you, Raymond. You shouldn't have run away. I caught eighteen." Lauren stretched her other leg. "Then I caught it big time when we got home."

"Yeah, Bash has to do our evening chores by himself tonight. Plus, he has to clean all the pie filling off the chickens." I shuddered. "I thought Aunt Tillie and Uncle Rollie would punish me too."

I watched Lauren hug one knee up to her chest. If I tried that, I'd topple over. I retied my shoelaces even though they weren't loose. "Maybe running is my punishment. They know I hate it." I rubbed my chin. "So that's why they wouldn't let me ground myself with a stack of comic books."

"They wanted to keep you boys apart so you couldn't come up with any more schemes."

"Hey, you and Bash wanted to stuff chickens in the trunk with the pies, not me."

"And now I'm stuck trying to teach a snail to run." Lauren stretched arms, hands still linked, palms upward, over her head. She eased them behind her. I got a cramp just watching. "Raymond, don't you exercise at home?"

"No way. Video games are safer."

"Video games make you fat."

"I'm not fat. These are Bash's sweatpants. I didn't bring any."

"Whatever." Lauren pointed up the road. "What if the robber jumps out at you? Are you going to waddle away like a duck?"

I shifted on the caveman rock. I hadn't thought about trying to get away from the robber. Running away beat catching him. "Well, maybe I should practice a little."

"Good. We'll run to the corner and back."

I squinted. I couldn't see the corner. "The next road's a mile away, isn't it?"

"Yep."

"So a mile up the road and a mile back. That's two miles."

"Very good. Next week, we'll test you on fractions."

I poked at my glasses. "You know what I mean. That's a long way."

"Not really." Lauren shaded her eyes. "The corner's up there somewhere, past the hayfield, the woods, and three or four other farms."

I groaned.

Lauren grabbed my arm and pulled me off my caveman easy chair. "Tell you what. We'll go with the beginner's plan. We'll run two minutes and walk four minutes."

"And that's a mile? Six minutes?"

"No, silly, that's the first cycle. We keep repeating sets of two and four minutes until we're back. It lets you build up slowly."

I shaded my eyes with my hands. The sun would set in almost two more hours. "Can we make it before dark?"

"Not if we keep standing here." Lauren spun on the balls of her feet and trotted to the side of the road. I shook one foot then the other.

Lauren hopped a couple times. "Ready? Go." She pushed a button on the powder blue stopwatch on her wrist and took off.

I ran beside her. "This is slow. Are we going too slowly? I can run faster. I really . . . can run . . . you know."

Lauren smiled. Her black hair swished as she loped. "Next set, Raymond. We're warming up."

I thought running would be hard. It was easy. Left foot, right foot, left foot, right foot. No big . . . deal. I inhaled deeply. Left foot, right foot. I gasped. Wait till Lauren saw how fast I could run the next set. Left foot. Right. Foot. I could keep this . . . up . . . all . . . day.

Lauren checked her watch. "One minute."

"Only . . . one?" I wheezed. Left . . . foot. . . . Right . . . foot . . . "Did the . . . *whooof* . . . watch . . . *phewpt* . . . stop?"

"Nope. It's fine. So how's school?"

"Isss . . . fiiiiiine . . ."

"Keep your head up, Raymond. You'll breathe better. And you need to watch for cars."

"Uh . . . huh . . ." Things looked blurry. I tapped my glasses to make sure they were still on.

Lauren hopped a couple steps. "Science class is my favorite. We're learning about plants. Photosynthesis is so cool. Did you learn about that yet?"

"*Urmp . . . ack.*"

"That's when plants soak in sunlight and turn it into energy, like little battery cells in iPods, and it—oh, two minutes and ten seconds. Time to walk."

I gasped. My side hurt. Maybe I had sat on the couch too much at home. "So the next road . . . *hufffff* . . . that's where . . . ugh . . . Clarey's Burgers and Cones is, isn't it?"

"Right. But we're not stopping. Mom said no ice cream for a week. Say, did you hear that the robber held up Clarey's yesterday?"

"He's early." What happened to "five or six days"?

"Mom told me this afternoon. The guy showed a gun in his pocket. He took everything in the cash register. Then he had them make a hot fudge sundae, with extra hot fudge, and extra whipped cream. He didn't pay even though he had a bag full of money."

"Wow." A hot fudge sundae with extra hot fudge sounded great. I didn't even need the extra whipped cream. Well, okay, maybe. "Did they catch him?"

"He got away. When we get to Clarey's, I'll help you look for clues."

"No clues . . . I'm not playing detective."

"Whatev." Lauren tossed her head back and inhaled. "Can you feel the energy, Raymond? I think we're photosynthesizing from the sun."

"I'd photosynthesize a hot fudge sundae." I got the whole sentence out without gasping.

"Not today. You're exercising."

"It's okay. Bash and I aren't allowed any dessert the rest of the week. Except some chicken-feather pie."

For the umpteenth time, Lauren peeked at the blue watch on her wrist. "Hey, it's almost four minutes. Get ready to run again."

"Your watch is broken. That can't be four minutes."

"I know. It feels like we've been walking forever. It's time to run again. Go."

I trotted beside Lauren. She talked. I tried to remember how to breathe.

"Isn't this fun, Raymond? I love getting out here. I love sprinting as fast as I can on the track. But I love the long runs too. I'm going to go out for cross country in the fall. Why don't you go out for cross country? You'll have all summer to work on your running. By fall, you'll be able to run three miles no problem. Did you ever get baptized?"

I stumbled. "How's . . . baptized . . . fit . . . with . . . cross . . . country?"

"It doesn't. Why? I just love having someone to talk to on long, slow runs. At church, they're talking about baptism. I haven't been baptized yet. I thought maybe you had."

"Is . . . that . . . *erk* . . . the . . . water . . . *mmmphhh* . . . thing?"

"Yeah. They dunk you in a tub of water. Or sometimes they do it in a pond. We could use Bash's pond. We could get baptized there."

"That's . . . *uffa, uffa, uffa* . . . called . . . *heff, heff* . . . swimming."

"Not diving in. Baptizing is when the pastor asks you if you believe in Jesus, and lowers you into the water, and brings you back up. Oh, two minutes. Walk time."

I walked. And wheezed. "Maybe . . . slower . . . next . . . time."

"I did pick up the pace on you a bit. I'm thinking maybe we better turn around at the half-mile mark. You don't look so well."

My lungs wanted to explode out of my chest. My right side ached. And I didn't want to run into any clues, guns, or robbers. "Let's . . . turn . . . a' half."

"So what about baptism? Have you done it?"

I shook my head, trying to switch gears with feet and topics. "No . . . must . . . have . . . forgot."

"See, I was reading the Farmin' and Fishin' Book—"

"Bible."

"Bash calls it the Farmin' and Fishin' Book, because it's all about farmers and fishermen. Did you know that God told Adam to take care of the Garden of Eden? The first man was the first farmer. And he farmed after God sent him and Eve out of the garden too."

"It's called . . . *oomph* . . . the Bible."

"But it's all about farmers and fishermen, and how God wants to plant good seeds in us, and weed out the bad stuff, and help us to grow fruit of the Spirit, and to be fishers of people to tell them about Jesus so they can be farmers too."

"Bible."

"Yeah, so anyway, in the Farmin' and Fishin' Book, just about as soon as somebody said they believed in Jesus as God's Son, some apostle or disciple tossed them into water. I remembered one of the verses."

Lauren squeezed her eyes shut and recited:

"'Repent,' Peter said to them, 'and be baptized, each of you, in the name of Jesus Christ for the forgiveness of your sins, and you will receive the gift of the Holy Spirit.'"

Lauren opened her eyes. "I found that in Acts 2:38. So what's it mean?"

I could almost talk now. "I'm not sure. I know we were saved when we asked Jesus to forgive us for all the wrong we did and asked Him to live inside our hearts. It felt like cold pond scum inside me before Jesus cleaned me up. But nobody threw me in water or splashed me or anything."

"I felt dark inside, and now it's light. So should we get baptized?"

"Isn't that just for important people? I'm not a preacher."

"Neither were most of the people in the Farmin' and Fishin' Book. Don't you want to be baptized?"

"I guess so. If that's what God wants us to do."

"Good. Let's do it. Four minutes. Run!"

My socks had turned into cement. I nearly tripped when a sneaker toe dragged on the roadside dirt. What was baptism? How come I couldn't pick up my feet? I needed to search in the back of my Bible where it lists topics to look up. How much longer before two minutes were up? My shirt felt baptized. Did I forget to do something Jesus wanted me to do? He'd tell me, right? Had it been two minutes yet?

I staggered into Lauren. "Sorry . . . When . . . can . . . *oofa, oofa* . . . we . . . walk . . . *huhhh, huhhhh* . . . again?"

"I am walking."

She was. Lauren walked. I ran and I couldn't keep up. "Can we . . . *uurp* . . . go home . . . *ullp* . . . now?"

"Let's turn here. We'll walk back. You can do this, Raymond. You'll love it like I do."

We crossed the road. Always face traffic when walking. Or waddling like a duck. What was wrong with me? When I spent last summer on the farm with Bash, I could run. Well, by the end of summer, anyway.

Lauren jogged circles around me. "Are you ready for tomorrow morning?"

"What's . . . *huffft* . . . tomorrow . . . morning?"

"April Fool's Day. Hasn't Bash told you the plan?"

"Nnn . . . no."

"It's awesome. You'll love it."

"Just like . . . *snnark* . . . I love . . . running?"

"Yep."

"Ugh. What's . . . plan?"

"He'll tell you."

I remembered why I wanted to practice running. I was going to need it to escape Mary Jane. And her goat. Maybe a robber with a gun. But that was my plan. Kind of. Bash's ideas are scarier. Lots scarier. I tried to remember all the things he said since I got here. I gulped.

"Lauren."

"Yeah?"

"We better do . . . another two minutes . . . of running."

Chapter 8

The Chocolate Closet

A thundering bull elephant shrieked a battle cry. If I didn't roll out of the way, I'd be as pulverized as peanut butter paste squished between elephant toes.

I rolled. "Bash, I'm going to throw your stupid alarm clock out the window if you don't *shut it off*!" I piled blankets and pillow over my head.

"C'mon, Beamer, get up, get up, *get up*! Today's the day the cows give chocolate milk."

I sighed. April Fool's Day already?

I pushed back the covers. A swarm of tiny, black spiders littered my pajamas and cascaded across the blankets.

I sighed. "Again?"

"April Fool!"

"You did the spider thing yesterday."

"Yeah, so today it's a surprise. You weren't expecting it twice. C'mon, get up. We've got lots of gags to pull."

I sat up and swatted plastic spiders across the floor. I slid into my slippers.

Schplooop!

"Surprise!"

I leaped back onto the bed and shook goopy slippers to the floor. "Really? And you guys call *me* boring? You can't even come up with new tricks."

Bash grinned. "This next one we're pulling on Pops is gonna be new. And you get to help."

I patted around the night stand for my glasses. Six a.m. comes way too early. I glanced at the now-silent screaming alarm clock. And nearly choked.

"Bash, it's *three*. In the *morning*. Not even the cows are up this early. Are you crazy? Don't answer that."

Bash flung open his closet door and dug through mounds of junk on the floor like a dog rooting out a mole. I ducked the stream of flying closet debris—socks, shirts, badminton rackets, Hot Wheels, books, and a bunch of other stuff.

"What are you doing, Digger Diggenstein?"

"Quiet, Beamer. You'll wake Ma and Pops. Ah, here they are."

Bash backed out of the closet, ten plastic jugs of Nestle

Nesquik chocolate drink powder clutched in his paws and tucked under his arms. "Take these."

"You're hoarding chocolate milk mix in your bedroom? You don't even have a refrigerator."

Bash crouched into his closet again and came up with six plastic jars of Ovaltine chocolate mix. "I've been planning this one since last year. Whenever I get enough allowance and birthday money, I buy another box from Mary Jane's store."

"It's still no good without a fridge. This stuff needs milk, you know."

Bash's blue eyes sparkled above a crooked grin. "Did you happen to notice that big building out back? The one with four-legged critters that go *moo*?"

Uh-oh.

Chief Strategist Bash put a finger to his lips. "Now quiet, Assistant Lackey Beamer. For the surprise to work, we gotta sneak out of the house."

We split up the boxes and jars of chocolate drink mix and crept down the stairs. The screen door groaned as Bash nudged it open at a snail's pace. "Shoulda oiled the spring last night," he whispered. "Careful. Don't let it slam."

We tiptoed down the driveway toward the barn.

"Bash."

"What?"

"Why are we still tiptoeing? We're outside."

"Oh, yeah. C'mon, let's go."

We started to run, but froze when a headlight hit us. I gaped into the single beam. The robber. Did he have his gun?

Where could I hide five boxes of Nesquik and two Ovaltines? Wait. If he wants chocolate milk mix, he could have it.

"Here!" I dropped Ovaltine and Nesquick boxes and bottles to the gravel driveway and held up my hands.

"Quit squeaking, and be quiet, Beamer." Bash trotted toward the herky-jerky headlight. "Cool. You made it."

"Of course, Pig Boy." Lauren hopped off her bicycle. The little headlight faded as she toed the kickstand into place. "This is going to be too good to miss."

Lauren's eyes glistened in the light over the barn door. She reached into the pockets of her silver blazer. Like pulling six-shooters from a cowboy holster, she whipped out a pair of brown bottles of Hershey's Syrup and aimed two barrels of chocolate nozzles at me. "Bang, bang, you're chocolate milk. You can put your hands down now."

"Huh? Oh." I dropped my arms and scooped my boxes and bottles from the driveway. "You're part of this?"

"Of course I am. Pig Boy told me about it last month. Mary Jane helped me buy the big bottles of syrup. There are four more in my book bag. She thinks we're all ridiculous, by the way."

Chief Strategist Bash nodded his head toward the barn. "'Course she does. She has no 'magination. She's never pulled a decent April Fool's joke in her life. C'mon, troops, let's go."

I looked around us into the hushed blackness and listened. "Bash, it's a curious thing that Uncle Jake did in the nighttime."

Bash slid open the barn door and headed toward the warmth of the milking parlor. "What is?"

"He didn't bark. He's still snoozing in his doghouse. Why didn't he bark when Lauren pedaled down the driveway?"

We hurried into the milk tank room where Lauren handed over her Hershey's bottles and dropped her book bag from the shoulders of her silver blazer. "Duh, Sherlock, he knows me. That's the significance of the silence of the dog."

"I guess. You're here all the time. Well, you live like next door almost. I'm stuck more than an hour away. By car. I'm not boring. I'm too far away. I can't just hop on my bike and pedal over anytime you guys do something fun. You can. Jig and Jag can. Bonkers. Even Mary Jane. Or walk. I could walk. No, that would take six weeks, maybe seven. I can be fun. If I could get here. You could call me. Oh, except I don't have my own cell phone yet. So you guys are together all the time, and I'm way over there in—*Ow!*" I rubbed my shoulder where Lauren slugged it.

She patted my head. "You're babbling, Raymond. You're cute when you're boring."

"That's not what I meant. It's just that, well, I dunno, I . . ."

The words ran out. Nuts. Whatever thought I meant to think probably was still in bed snoring. I should be in bed snoring with my thoughts. I sucked in a deep breath, filling my nose with the sweet scent of sanitizer and milk fumes. The humming of the refrigerated milk tank swelled in my ears. I blew the air out slowly and tried to shake myself awake.

I picked up a jug of Hershey's Syrup. "I'm in. What are we supposed to do with the chocolate stuff, anyway?"

Chief Strategist Bash lined up the jugs, jars, and bottles on the windowsill and on upside-down five-gallon buckets. "You'll see. We're almost ready. Now we just need—"

The parlor door crashed open. A dark, snarling, hunch-backed monster thundered into the room. I dropped the syrup bottle. Somebody screamed.

We were going to die.

"Knock off the screaming, Beamer. You'll wake the dog." Bonkers slung a bulky backpack off his shoulders and let it thud to the floor. I jumped again.

"I set my alarm . . . *huff, huff* . . . so low that even I didn't hear it right away. *Huff, huff.* Good thing I've got good night vision. I ran . . . *huff, huff* . . . all the way here." Bonkers leaned over and gasped in a few big breaths.

Hey, at not much past three a.m., anybody could have mistaken wheezing and panting like that for a monster's snarls. Is that how horrible I sounded running with Lauren yesterday? If I snarled like I was Hulking out, why didn't it make me run faster?

While Bonkers gasped, I thumped my chest to start my heart beating again. "You too? Bash, can just anybody sneak up on us without Uncle Jake barking?"

Bash pulled more boxes of Nesquik from Bonkers's book bag. "Uncle Jake O'Rusty McGillicuddy Junior only barks at people he doesn't know. He didn't bark at you either."

"He did when I first got here."

"That was barking hello. He slurped your face too."

"Well . . ."

"C'mon, we gotta make chocolate milk."

Bonkers added eight more jugs of Nesquik, three bottles

each of Ovaltine and Hershey's, and two bottles of Yoo-hoo chocolate drink to the lineup. He popped open one of the Yoo-hoos, gulped, and wiped his mouth on his sleeve. "I've been buying chocolate mix from Morris's store ever since you told me about it last year. By the way, Mary Jane thinks it's insane—"

"Mary Jane just likes boring stuff, that's all."

I peeked out the window. Nothing but night. "What next? Are Jig and Jag going to show up too? How will we know? The dog doesn't bark."

Bash shook his head. "Nope. They're little kids. It's too dark for nine-year-olds."

"It's too dark for me, too, but you dragged me out here."

Lauren grabbed my arm. "It's exciting, isn't it, Raymond? Unless you're afraid of the dark."

I snapped myself up as tall and fierce as possible. "And I am not afraid of . . . *Aaaaugh!*"

The door crashed open. Two fire-headed trolls charged into the room.

"*Jig. Jag.* You came." Bash plunked Jig in the shoulder. "Don't mind Beamer. He's scared of the dark."

My hands on Lauren's shoulders, I peeked up from behind her and squeaked, "Am not."

The twins Jig and Jag, their green eyes dancing between fields of freckles and splashes of bright orange hair, fidgeted book bags off scrawny shoulders.

I let go of Lauren and jumped back. She arched an eyebrow at me. "You were saying, o brave warrior?"

"I'm not afraid of the dark. But that robber you guys keep talking about makes me nervous."

Lauren grinned. "He only comes out in the daylight. Some people are afraid of the dark, you know. You and the robber will have lots in common to talk about when you catch him, Holmes."

"I'm not playing detective." I pointed out the window. "They got me by surprise. Uncle Jake didn't warn us. Besides, Bash said they were too young to be out in the dar— to be out this early."

Jag snorted. "We turn ten in eleven days. My birthday is twelve minutes before Jig's."

Jig crossed his arms. "It's the same day. It doesn't mean you're older. I don't have to listen to you."

Jag locked and loaded one of her sharp elbows. "You better, *little* brother."

Jig shook his head. "Nuh-uh. We're twins. Same age."

Jag snorted. She was about to snap off another remark— and maybe an elbow to the ribs—but Bash interrupted. "So whatchya got?"

Jig yanked his book bag closer. "We've been saving up chocolate milk stuff like you said. We got it at Mary Jane's store."

Jag unzipped her bag. "MJ says you're goofy gopher brains for thinking this will work."

Bash unzipped Jig's book bag. "Mary Jane eats gophers for breakfast. With sour lemonade."

Bash, Jig, and Jag unloaded another six jars of Nesquik, two Hershey's bottles, one Ovaltine, and four boxes of chocolate Jell-O pudding mix. Bash and Bonkers ran out the door, came back with a couple planks, and plunked them across upside-down five-gallon pails. They lined up the boxes, jars, jugs, and bottles of chocolate across the plank like a shelf in a crazy chocolate mix store.

Chief Strategist Bash paced from end to end of the chocolate shelf. "This looks great. It's gotta be enough."

I straightened the jugs and jars so they lined up evenly, like on store shelves. "For what? The sugar buzz of the century?"

"'Course not." Bash skidded to a stop in front of my nose. He rubbed his hands together like a mad scientist. And cackled. "Beamer, we're about to make the cows give chocolate milk."

Chapter 9

Parlor Tricks

Bash pulled a calculator from his back pocket. "Okay, we have sixty-three cows, but seven of them aren't milkers, so that makes . . ." He tapped the keypad.

"Fifty-six," I said. "And you can't make cows give chocolate milk."

Bash punched one more button. ". . . fifty-six milk cows. Good. Let's see, each cow averages about eight gallons of milk a day, so that's eight gallons times fifty-six cows . . ." Bash chewed his tongue and stabbed more buttons.

"It's 448." I sighed. "I don't care how much powder and syrup you feed them, cows won't milk chocolate. Not the brown ones. Not the red ones. Not the black-and-white ones."

Bonkers and Lauren began twisting lids off the jars. Bash tapped the keys. ". . . equals 448. Okay, the morning milking will be about half, which is . . ."

"Half of 448 is 224, Bash." I tapped my foot. "Are you listening to me?"

". . . yeah, right, 224 gallons. But last night's milking is still here in the bulk tank since the milk truck comes in the afternoon. So 224 gallons last night plus 224 gallons this morning adds up to . . ."

Bonkers took another swig of Yoo-hoo. Lauren shook her head. Bash tapped keys. I leaned against the whitewashed block wall. "It's too early in the morning for jokes, Bash. You know it's 448."

I thought I caught Bash winking at Bonkers. Either that, or he squinted at the screen. ". . . Ha! Just as I suspected. It's 448 gallons of milk. Okay, one glass of chocolate milk is eight ounces, and there are sixty-four ounces in a gallon. So each gallon contains six glasses—"

"Eight. If they could."

"—eight glasses of milk. So to find out how many glasses of chocolate milk 448 gallons adds up to, let's see, carry the four . . ." *Tap, tap, tap.* "No, wait, it's pi squared, plus tax, cake cubed, minus the scoring average of the Cleveland Cavaliers point guard, carry the zero . . ." *Tap, tap, tap.*

I clamped both hands to my temples and squeezed. "It's 3:30. In the morning."

". . . plus 330 . . ." *Tap, tap, tap.*

I plugged my ears. "Stop tapping the keys. Just multiply 448 by eight, Bash."

"Thanks, Assistant Lackey Beamer. I knew I'd get you to tell me. Okay four . . ." *Tap.* ". . . four . . ." *Tap.* ". . . eight . . ." *Tap.* ". . . times . . ." *Tap.*

"That would be 3,584 glasses of milk," I said. "Can't you do math in your head?"

"Why? I'm the brains of this outfit. You do the math."

Bonkers snickered. Lauren grinned. I clunked my head against the wall.

Bash grabbed a chunk of chalk and screeched the number 3,584 at the bottom of a blackboard hanging on the milk house wall.

"Now we gotta figure out how much chocolate we have." He handed me one of the plastic jars of Nesquik. "Check the labels for numbers of servings, and see if we've got enough to make 3,584 glasses of chocolate milk."

"Where are you going to get 3,584 glasses? Even if you gather up all the glasses, cups, coffee mugs, candle holders, and your sister's sippy cups, you can't pull together 3,584 glasses at 3:30 in the morning."

"We don't need glasses. We've got this." Chief Strategist Bash *boinged* his knuckles against the bulk tank that looked like a slightly smaller version of an oil tanker truck.

Oh, no. The brain fog cleared from the chocolate cobwebs in my head. "You can't be serious. We're not pouring chocolate powder into the milk tank. That'll—"

Bash jammed his fists into his hips and stuck out his chest in a Superman pose. "Yep. The milking machines attach to the cows' udders. The warm milk squirts into tubes. The tubes whoosh the white stuff across the parlor. Gallons and gallons of milk splash down inside the tank. It's like a giant refrigerator, with a stir stick inside. Add powder and syrup, stir, and guess what you've got?"

"Trouble?" I shook my head. "So when the dairy truck guy comes for pickup . . ."

"Yep, he sees that the cows milked chocolate. It will be totally awesome."

I slapped my forehead. "We are so grounded. Again."

Bonkers scratched his head. "Why? Kids love chocolate milk. Grown-ups too."

Bash nodded. "The dairy company'll probably give Pops an extra premium on today's milking. He's gonna think it's the best prank ever. We'll be heroes."

I shook my head. "Champions of April Fool's Day."

"Yepper. Makes you proud, doesn't it?"

Lauren tapped the Nesquik I held. "So c'mon, Raymond. Do the math. Are we good?"

"I don't think any of this is good."

"Sure it is. An' it's not boring. You wanna stay stuck at boring all your life?"

I squinted at a label. "Let's see, the Nesquik is about eighty-five servings a jar, and we have—six, eight, ten, twelve, fourteen, eighteen, twenty—twenty-four jars, so that's twenty-four times eighty-five . . ."

I stared at a flake of peeling whitewash in the far corner where the wall met the ceiling and tried to work it out. I can't do math when I'm nervous. "Basher, give me the calculator."

I tapped keys. Hit the wrong ones. Cleared entry. Tried again. "That's 2,040 glasses. Hand me an Ovaltine. Um, forty-six servings a jar . . ." I added in the Ovaltine. Bash screeched the number on the chalk board.

"The Hershey's. Each big bottle has . . . there it is, about thirty-five servings, so . . ."

I pecked more keys. Bash paced circles, Jig following in his wake. Bonkers, Lauren, and Jag peeked over my shoulders, getting in each other's way because there were three of them to my two shoulders.

I tapped more keys. "Add to the Hershey's, the Ovaltine, and Nesquik totals . . ."

I hit the *equals* button. Lauren groaned. Bonkers backed away. Jag snorted. Bash stopped so suddenly that Jig ran into his back. Bash didn't seem to notice. "What? *What?*"

I turned the calculator his direction. "You've got enough here for 2,780 servings. You're 804 glasses short."

Bash slumped. "A whole year. A whole year of planning. An' we're still short." He picked up a bottle of syrup and balanced it in his palm. He frowned. "Rats."

I jumped. "Where?"

"No, I mean 'rats' like 'bummer.' It's not enough."

"Plus the pudding mix."

"It won't work."

I studied the big, hulking bulk tank that stored the milk of all the cows. "You could make light chocolate milk."

"Like diet chocolate milk?" His eyes sparkled like blue firecracker fuses. "Beamer, you saved April Fool's Day."

Something warmed my chest. "Thanks. See, I'm not boring." Then ice choked the warm spot. "But let's not tell your folks that I'm a hero, okay?"

"Why not? They're gonna love—"

The milking parlor door whipped open again. This time, Bash dropped the bottle of syrup. Somebody screamed. I hoped it wasn't me again.

Mary Jane burst into the milk house. "Did Sebastian Nicholas Hinglehobb mess things up yet?"

I peeled myself off the wall. I really wished the dog would bark in the night.

Bash scooped up the chocolate bottle. "Mary Jane. What are you doing here?"

She dropped a backpack to the floor. "You little kids with your little kid allowances couldn't possibly buy enough chocolate powder to pull off your little stunt. I've been getting Mom and Dad to order extra all year and put some aside myself."

Bash picked up Mary Jane's pink backpack and nearly dropped it. He set it down, pulled back the zipper, and reached inside. He pulled out a bottle. And another. And another.

Bash grinned. Bonkers cheered. Lauren giggled. The twins whooped. Even I snickered.

From Mary Jane's bag, Bash unpacked eight big containers of Nesquik, four bottles of Hershey's, two Ovaltines, and two Betty Crocker chocolate cake mixes.

Bash pointed an Ovaltine at me. "Assistant Lackey Beamer, the math."

"Already on it." I ignored the cake boxes since I didn't know how to count them for milk mix. I smacked buttons for the rest and held up the calculator for the gang to see. "Ladies and gentlemen, behold. We now have enough stuff to stir up 3,692 big, cold glasses of chocolate milk. We are 108 glasses over."

Bash pumped his fist. "Yesssss. Mary Jane, you saved April Fool's Day."

Mary Jane yawned. "Not hard when a goofball is in charge."

"You're the best when it comes to Fool's."

"Watch it, Sebastian Nicholas Hinglehobb."

"I wasn't calling you a fool. I meant you're the Queen of Fool's Da—"

"Stop while you're only this far behind." Mary Jane unscrewed the lid from one of the Hershey's bottles. "Every day is Weirdos Day around here."

I tossed Bash his calculator. "I thought you said that *I* saved April Fool's Day."

"Yeah, but you're . . . Ah, forget it." Chief Strategist Bash climbed the little ladder attached to the end of the refrigeration tank and popped open the lid. "Hand me the first bottle of chocolate mix."

Jig stumbled toward the bottles. "I'll do it!" He grabbed a big jug of Nesquik mix, held it high, and leaped toward Bash, who snagged it.

Bash tipped the jar over the tank lid. "Fire one."

Bottle by jar by jug by canister, Bonkers, Lauren, Jig and Jag, and even Mary Jane handed chocolate ammo up to Bash.

Kalump. The contents of a big box of powder whumped into the milk tank. "Pops'll probably wonder why he didn't think of this." *Splllooooootttt. Skynxx.* Syrup burped out of a bottle. "It's genius."

I kept watch out the window and saw only one thing—night. "Hurry up, guys."

Lauren handed up another Hershey's bottle. "Last one."

Bash tipped the bottle and thick, brown syrup *glug-glug-glugged* into the tank. "Down the hatch. That's it. We're done."

Bash slammed the tank lid shut, latched the seal, and hopped off the platform. "Okay, everybody gather up their empty bottles. We don't want anyone to find out until the milk truck comes at about four in the afternoon. This will be so stupendously epic."

The kids crammed bottles and jars into their book bags. I wiped chocolate drips off the slopes of the tank walls. "We might as well head on up to your room at two. It'll save your folks the trouble of grounding us."

Bash picked up the planks and stacked the empty pails in place. "Why would they ground us? Chocolate milk straight from the cows. Almost. We'll be April Fool's heroes. Now scatter."

We doused the lights and slipped out of the milking parlor. After watching the last bicycle disappear down the driveway darkness, Bash and I ran for the back door.

"*Woof, woof, woof, woof!*"

"*Shh!* It's us, Uncle Jake."

The dog finally barked in the nighttime. Doom for the April Fool's heroes.

Chapter 10

Pasted Oreos and Salted Coffee

We made it inside the house and upstairs without waking Uncle Rollie and Aunt Tillie. Uncle Jake's howling lasted another couple minutes after we dived back under the bedcovers.

"He's going to spoil the surprise," Bash whispered.

With the dog wailing, my nerves jangling, my knees knocking, and my chest heaving, it took nearly two whole minutes before I fell asleep.

And two minutes after that—so it seemed—a pack of hyenas laughed, slobbered, and snarled circles around my slumber.

I was so throwing that zoo alarm clock out the window.

I pulled the covers over my head. It didn't work. I still heard Bash. "C'mon, Beamer, get up, get up, *get up*! Today's the day the cows give chocolate milk."

Didn't he say that just a couple minutes ago, right before we went out to the barn, and . . .

I whipped back the covers, spraying plastic black spiders everywhere. "Basher, please tell me I just had a bad dream. Tell me we didn't pour chocolate milk mix in the bulk tank."

Bash hopped around the room as he pulled on his sneakers. "We sure did. And there's more awesomeness to come."

I squinted at the alarm clock. Six in the morning. I untangled two plastic spiders from my hair. "This is super lame. You can't pull the same dumb trick a couple hours apart."

"What trick?" He snickered. "Okay, okay, you're too smart for me."

"I know." I sat up and swished plastic spiders across the floor. I slid off the bed into my slippers.

Schplooop!

"Not the mint shaving cream in the slippers *again*." I groaned. "There's more shaving cream than slipper."

The Basher fell across his bed and nearly choked with laughter. "Strike three!"

I threw two goopy slippers at him. One splatted onto the wall behind him and stuck. The other splotched him in the middle of his T-shirt. Bash peeled off the slipper, squeezed a blob of shaving cream into his palm, and flung it. Mint cream exploded across my face.

"Now you're in for it, buster." I dove across the room for the slipper gooped to the wall. *Splllump*. It pulled loose. *Splaaack*. I gunked Bash with slippered shaving cream across his back as he tried to roll out of the way.

"Oh, you're gonna get it now." Bash jumped slipper-first for my nose. *Thwap*.

We rolled around in splats and giggles, gobs of shaving cream splattering everywhere with each direct hit until the slippers ran dry.

"*Boys!* Breakfast!" Aunt Tillie bellowed up the stairs.

We rolled away from each other. "Now *that's* the way to start the day." Bash grinned through a mug full of shaving cream.

We checked on the tadpoles and froglets. Bash pressed his nose to the glass. "We're gonna have some hoppers soon. Lookit those guys holding themselves up outta the water on the rocks an' sticks."

Longer legs and shorter tails sprouted from the ones Bash pointed at. Others still looked blobby and squiggled through the water on swishy tails and leg nubbins.

"That's amazing. The ugly blobs really are turning into handsome frogs."

We turned from the tank and glooped and glopped our way to the kitchen, where Aunt Tillie shoveled fried eggs off a griddle. I inhaled the wondrous scents of morning in the farmhouse—buttery-peppered eggs, maple-spiced sausages, sizzling-salted bacon, and the sweet crispness of Aunt Tillie's homemade strawberry-rhubarb jam on warm toast. Why else would anyone stumble out of bed at this awful hour of the morning?

Uncle Rollie burbled steaming coffee into a mug and set it on the table. "By jingle juniper jangles, that smells like morning." He washed his hands at the kitchen sink, winked at me, and crept up behind Bash, one cupped hand dripping water.

Uncle Rollie held the cupped hand to his lips and faked a sneeze. *"Ahh-CHOO!"* The "sneeze" splattered Bash's hair with a misty shower of "snot."

I about choked on my glass of milk.

"Pops, *no*." Bash shook his head like Uncle Jake after coming in from the rain. "I was gonna get Beamer with that one."

"Sorry about that, Chief." Uncle Rollie wiped his hand with a red paisley handkerchief and jammed the wadded-up hanky into his back overalls pocket. "Oh, hey, special treat today. I had to run up to Morris's store yesterday, so I picked up a package of Oreos. Cookies with your breakfast, anyone?"

Bash shook his head. "None for me today, Pops. I'll brush after breakfast."

I didn't know what brushing had to do with anything, but when a grown-up says you can eat chocolate cookies before dessert, you better grab them before he changes his mind. "Sure, thanks." I pulled five Oreos from the open package. "Can we start now?"

Uncle Rollie fiddled with his mustache. "Abso-posi-lutely, Ray. Dig in."

I bit into the chocolate and crème goodness—and gagged. *"Ptwooie."* I spit soggy cookie pieces onto my plate. "What is this? Baking soda flavor?"

Uncle Rollie chuckled. "It's good for what ails you."

Bash high-fived Uncle Rollie across the table. "Ya got 'im, Pops." Bash picked up a cookie and unscrewed the top. "It's toothpaste."

I grabbed my glass of milk with both hands and chugged. "Blech. What happened to the crème filling?"

Uncle Rollie smacked his lips. "Tasted dandier than dollar doughnuts. Happy April Fool's Day, Ray."

"He hasn't caught me with that one since I was three." Bash nudged the sugar bowl toward the center of the table. "Sugar for your coffee, Pops?"

"No, I've a hankering for salt today." Uncle Rollie tightened the wobbly lid on the shaker, and salted his coffee. He sipped the brew and sighed. "Ahh. Just the way I like it." Another sip. "You're going to have to get up awfully early in the morning if you're aiming to make me your April Fool, buddy boy."

Aunt Tillie dropped three slices of bacon on each plate, placed a platter with the rest of it on the table, and sat down. She reached for the salt and pepper shakers, and checked to make sure the lids weren't loosened. "We'll have none of your shenanigans, no matter what the calendar says. Now let's say grace so we can eat."

Uncle Rollie thanked God for farm, family, and food. At "amen," we dug in.

"Pass the salt, please."

"Sure, Ma."

Aunt Tillie sprinkled her eggs, took a big bite—and spit it out. "What in the world?"

Bash burst into laughter. Uncle Rollie grinned. "Sugar in the salt shaker. I believe he got you with that one last year, Mattie."

Uncle Rollie always calls her Mattie. Everyone else calls her Tillie. Mom says her real name's Matilda. Weird.

Aunt Tillie's eyelid ticked. "April Fool's Day with you and your dad makes me a nervous wreck."

Uncle Rollie clucked his tongue. "You shouldn't get so worked up, honeybunches. It's good, clean fun. Here, let me get those egg specks for you." He pulled another handkerchief from a different pocket, and carefully wiped spluttered egg bits from Aunt Tillie's face. When he was done, big, inky blotches circled each of her cheeks and the tip of her nose, and her forehead sported the word "Hi!" smudged backwards.

I gasped. Uncle Rollie winked. Bash caught my eye and put a finger to his lip. Aunt Tillie didn't notice as she busied herself scraping sugar off her eggs. "Thanks, sweetheart."

I tried hard not to stare at Aunt Tillie's tattooed face. Instead, I stared at the eggs on my plate. I sliced open the yolks with my fork, and watched yellow goo run across the fried whites. Phew. The eggs weren't rubber. You never know around this place.

Uncle Rollie reached for the massive, worn-out Bible with the duct-taped spine that he always brought to breakfast. My mom and dad call me in for family devotions just before bedtime. Bash's family reads from God's Word and prays around the breakfast table.

Uncle Rollie crammed the last of his toast into his mouth, pressed a flap of duct tape back into place, and flipped crinkled Bible pages. "We're just going to look at four verses today, Philippians 4:4–7: 'Rejoice in the Lord always. I will say it again: Rejoice! Let your graciousness be known to everyone. The Lord is near. Don't worry about anything, but in everything, through prayer and petition with thanksgiving, let your requests be made known to God. And the peace of God, which surpasses every thought, will guard your hearts and minds in Christ Jesus.'"

The cover nearly slid off when Uncle Rollie closed the Bible. "Guys, that bandit seems to be hanging around here somewhere. But like our reading today says, we don't have to worry about anything."

Well that just shot up my worry meter sixteen notches.

Bash pointed his fork. "It's okay. Detective Beamer's gonna catch the robber."

"Am not." I turned on Uncle Rollie. "What's that 'don't worry' part? You guys have a robber running around the township. Are you just supposed to say, 'Thank You, Lord, that some crazy guy with a gun wants to take all my money, and maybe shoot me too'?"

"The Bible tells us many times to prepare, to watch, and to be ready. But we can't just hide under the bed all day. Here, check out this verse." Uncle Rollie flipped open the Bible, found a page, and smoothed out a crinkle. "Remember Psalm 23, the one that starts, 'The LORD is my shepherd.'"

Bash's hand shot up. "The farmers' song."

Uncle Rollie chuckled. "You could say that." His finger moved down the page. "Verse 4 says, 'Even when I go through the darkest valley, I fear no danger, for You are with me.' And over here in Psalm 56:3–4, it says, 'When I am afraid, I will trust in You. In God, whose word I praise, in God I trust; I will not fear. What can man do to me?'"

"He can shoot me."

Aunt Tillie daubed sugar off her eggs. "But God still holds your heart in His hand." Aunt Tillie's eyelid ticked. She spooned white stuff from the sugar bowl, sniffed at it, and "sugared" her eggs. "Look, we're not used to this kind of thing going on out here. But we want you boys to know you can trust God. And we want you to stay safe. Stay together, and let us know where you're at."

I unscrewed a cookie top off an Oreo, scraped it against my plate to wipe away the baking soda toothpaste filling, and poked the pasteless cookie into my mouth. "If God loves us, why's He let trouble come?"

"So we grow stronger and learn how much we can trust Him. Let's go back to Philippians." Uncle Rollie turned a chunk of pages. "It says 'don't worry about anything, but in everything, through prayer and petition with thanksgiving, let your request be made known to God.' See, God's our Father. If something's bothering us, He wants us to tell Him."

Aunt Tillie sighed. "I talk to God about you boys all the time."

Uncle Rollie chuckled. "It's like running. You won't run faster and longer by picking out shoelaces, no matter how spiffy-sporty they are. You have to pick up your feet and go."

Uncle Rollie sipped his coffee. "First you walk, building your wind up. Then you run a little. More than likely, you wheeze worse than a rattletrap tractor on its last legs. But you get faster, you run longer. Finally, you find out you can *run*. And you discover you grew healthier and stronger with all the practice."

I shuffled the toothpaste Oreos through the rest of devotions and prayer. I hated running. And not worrying about a nut with a gun robbing people didn't seem smart. Sure, I believed God, but didn't He want me to do something too? Like hide under the bed? Maybe the next time the robber tried to hold up somebody, they should give him Oreos with baking soda toothpaste, and—

"Ray."

"Huh? What? I was listening."

Uncle Rollie chuckled. "I said, I reckon we boys ought to get started."

"Oh. Yeah. Okay."

Uncle Rollie scraped his chair away from the table and pulled one of his hankies out of his pocket. "Here, honey pie, I missed a spot." He reached over the table and tenderly wiped Aunt Tillie's cheek. Then he kissed her right on the lips.

"Gross!" Bash yelped. "We just ate."

Aunt Tillie grinned. "Well, I think it's sweet. Haven't you ever seen a husband kiss his wife before?"

What I'd never seen before was the heart he'd drawn on Aunt Tillie's cheek. At least it wasn't backwards like the word "Hi!" smudged on her forehead. Well, maybe it was. You can't really tell about hearts.

Uncle Rollie poked the handkerchief back in his pocket. "Hurry up, boys. I suspect we ought to get out to the barn soon."

Bash nodded. "Yeah, that would be good."

We barely made it thirty paces before a shriek curdled the air from the direction of the bathroom window. *"Rollllll-laaaaaaaand!"* It sounded like a freshly tattooed Aunt Tillie just read Uncle Rollie's forehead greeting in the mirror. I wondered if she saw the heart forward or backward.

Uncle Rollie quickened his steps and winked at Bash. "If your ma keeps bellowing like that, she's going to wake Darla an hour early. By the way, I wore my other boots, so you can clean the Jell-O out of my regular ones after barn duties. Yep, you gotta get up awfully early in the morning to get your ol' dad, champ. Awfully early."

Chapter 11

Eggs in Flight

Uncle Rollie clucked his tongue at the "Use Other Side" sign taped to the single barn door. "Great Granny's gravy, son, you've got to stop using your Spider-Man tape if you expect to fool anyone with the fake sign trick."

Uncle Rollie wrapped beefy fingers around the edge of the wooden door and slid it open. "I reckon you'll want to use hot water and plenty of soap to clean the Vaseline off the door handle. You've got to get up pretty early in the morning to prank me. Get the lights, will you?"

"I don't think so, Pops. Let Beamer."

My knees buckled. Bash had just refused a direct order from his dad. He was in for it now, unless I did something fast. I hurried to the light box and flicked the switch. Only the switch didn't flick. I tried again. I couldn't notch my finger under the flicker.

I held my breath. Looked at the switch. Spider-Man tape. Plastered all over the light switch.

Bash cackled. Uncle Rollie shook his head. "Yep, pretty early in the morning."

I clawed the tape off the switch. Craziness. I'd be safer hiding under the bed until April 2.

Bash nudged me. "Get the shovel and scrape the floor behind the cows."

"How come I have to shovel the smelly gunk again?"

"'Cause I'm getting the wheelbarrow." Bash ran. I sighed and shuffled to the barn shovel.

Uncle Rollie toted a stack of watering buckets to the faucet and turned on the tap. I listened to water pound into the pails while I scrunched my nose, held my breath, and cleaned cow stalls.

"*Rrrrrrrr, rrrrrrrr!*" Bash wailed like a siren as he zigged and zagged at me with the wheelbarrow. "Load the patients in the ambulance, Beamer."

I slung a shovel full of "patients" toward the "ambulance." The ambulance zigged, or possibly zagged. Half the load splattered to the concrete floor.

"You've got to have better aim than that." Rescue Ranger Bash swerved but splonked into the clump of gunk on the floor. The wheelbarrow shuddered. Then the single wheel popped off. The ambulance *ka-chunked* to the floor. Bash toppled over the handles and became a patient in his own ambulance. *Splat!*

"Yuck!" Rescue Ranger Bash rescued himself from his ambulance, shaking goop off his arms.

Uncle Rollie hurried over with one of the water buckets. "I wonder how that loose wheel picked such a fine time to leave you. Here, let me wash you off." He hoisted the pail and took aim.

Bash stood Superman style, fists on hips, chest out. Uncle Rollie whipped the watering bucket. A flurry of straw exploded out of the bucket and trickled all over the Basher.

Bash blew out a mouthful of the straw. "*Pffft*. Ha! I knew all along you didn't have water in the bucket."

Uncle Rollie winked. "Maybe so, scarecrow. But I still gotcha. You've been tarred and feathered. Happy April Fool's Day, kidling o' mine."

Oh, my. I'd never been so relieved as when we finally finished our cow barn chores and escaped to the refuge of the chicken coop.

As usual, Bash beat me to the feed sack, leaving me with the broom and the messy work. As usual, Lizzie Longhorn Leghorn chicken-strutted around me and flap-dashed between my legs, pecking at the tops of my sneakers. "*Ow.* She pecked a hole right through the canvas."

Bash scattered crushed corn chicken feed in the trough. "Your toes look like worms."

"Do not."

"Chickens eat bugs and stuff. The chickens always peck your toes. That means your toes look like worms. Or maybe potato bugs."

I swept chicken glop and gunky feathers into a pile. "Yeah, well, your face looks like a weasel."

"Weasels are cool. Hurry up and collect the eggs, wormy Beamy. We're gonna play a great gag on Ma."

Speaking of weasels . . .

After popping open pop doors to let the hens spend the day pecking through the yard, and after feeding and mucking the hogs, we trudged inside and cleaned two dozen eggs—the morning's collection—and our stinky selves in the mudroom sink.

Aunt Tillie handed us two empty egg cartons. "Pack the eggs carefully. Your pa will deliver them to the neighbors who wanted them on his way to the grist mill."

"Sure thing, Ma. See how gently I'm placing the eggs?"

"Just don't crack any shells this time." Aunt Tillie headed toward the living room to check on Darla.

Commando Cracked-Egg Bash dashed to the doorway and peeked around the corner. "She's out of sight. Let's do it."

I poked my glasses and looked around. "Do what?"

Bash picked up one of the egg cartons. "Throw my barn jacket in that pail. That'll be soft enough. Help me unload these eggs."

We emptied the carton into the padded pail. Bash closed the lid. A grin crooked across his face. Mad sparkles fairly burst from his blue eyes. He crouched toward the open door. My stomach prickled like flying downhill on a roller coaster. I needed to run.

Bash waved me to follow. "Okay, troops, commence Operation Egg Fright."

We tiptoed through the kitchen. Commando Bash peeked

into the dining room. He motioned for me to follow. We crept across the floor. At the archway to the living room, Commando Cracked Egg held up the hand not clutching the carton. "On my mark, men. Let's go."

I nodded, then realized I had no clue what to do. "Um, Bash—"

Too late. The commando attacked. With a whoop, he charged into the living room, where Aunt Tillie sat in her rocking chair reading a book to Darla. "Hey, Ma, where do want me to set aside this carton for—*oops.*"

Bash tripped. He overdid the acting, tripping over nothing but air. Aunt Tillie was too busy concentrating on Bash's scrambling feet and flailing arms—and the egg carton—to notice. Bash tumbled through an exaggerated somersault and crashed in a heap against the living room wall. The carton flew toward the ceiling.

Aunt Tillie shrieked. Her bulging eyes locked onto the egg carton, shuddering in midair at the ceiling level and tilting downward. Aunt Tillie blasted out of her rocking chair, whisked Darla off her lap and into the rocker seat, and dove like an outfielder toward the toppling carton.

She'd calculated her aim based on the speed a dozen dive-bombing eggs would smash to the floor in big, gooey gushes.

The empty carton fluttered and flip-flopped, taking its time to fall.

The box bopped Aunt Tillie's backside as she slid past, arms outstretched.

Over the smoldering scent of fresh rug burn, Commando Cracked Egg Bash cackled, "April Fool! Gotcha, Ma!"

Next thing I knew, Aunt Tillie held the empty egg carton in one hand and Bash in the other. I'd rather not remember what happened next.

Sometime later in the mudroom, Bash held the remains of the egg carton while I pulled the eggs from the pail and packed them into a fresh carton. "I don't think your mom liked your gag."

Commando Cracked-Egg Bash grinned. "She will. Later. When her ladies' missionary group meets this month, she'll tell them all about it. She'd have nothing to report without me."

I placed the last egg in the carton. "Maybe she'd like that."

"Why? That would be boring. A couple ladies say they only show up to hear what I did this time. I tell you, Ray-Ray Sunbeam Beamer, sometimes it's hard to come up with new stuff."

"Seems pretty easy for you. Except for that stupid name you keep calling me. Stop calling me that."

Bash closed the carton lid, stacked it on top of the other full one, and carried them toward the door. "Get that coffee mug, Beamer."

I snatched a red and yellow mug from a metal coat locker. The cup pulled back before letting go. I peered at its underside. "Bash, somebody glued magnets on the bottom of this thing."

"Yeah. I'm gonna put it on the roof of Pop's truck just before he leaves so it looks like he left his mug on the cab. People will honk at him all the way to the grist mill, and he won't know why. It'll be great."

"You're a doofus."

Uncle Rollie waited in the pickup truck loaded with sacks of corn and oats to be hauled to the mill to be ground into grain. I hid the mug behind my back while Bash handed Uncle Rollie the egg cartons through the open window. "Here ya go, Pops."

"Thanks, Champ." When Uncle Rollie turned to place the eggs on the seat beside him, Bash grabbed the mug and plunked it atop the cab. It held.

"Okay, Pops, see you later. You'll be back before the milk truck gets here, right?"

I groaned. Uncle Rollie tipped his cap. "Yep. Now don't pester the stuffing out of your ma. Leave your April Fooling for me. If you think you can get me."

"Sure, Pops."

The truck started to pull away. Then stopped. Uncle Rollie opened the cab door, reached up, plucked the mug from the roof, and looked inside. "You could have at least filled it with coffee." He shrugged and tossed the mug inside the truck. "Not early enough in the morning, young grasshopper."

Uncle Rollie drove away. I etched lines through the driveway gravel with a sneaker toe. "He knew. Maybe you shouldn't have left it in the mudroom where he could see it."

"It's all part of the plan. Pops thinks we're still trying. He doesn't know he's already been got."

I slumped against a maple tree at the edge of the drive. "Yeah, the milk truck. I can hardly wait. Should we start running away from home now or wait until your mom and dad are chasing us?"

"Neither. It's time to go paint Mary Jane's goat."

Chapter 12

Getting Mary Jane's Goat

The dread weighed more than the book bag slung over my shoulders. "We're really going to get Mary Jane's goat?"

Bash scooted behind me. I heard the *zzzzzzt* of the zipper and felt the *ka-thunks* of stuff dropping on top of the cans of spray-on hair coloring. Bash announced each *ka-thunk*: "Chalk from the Space Shuttle Sebastian." *Ka-thunk.* "Watercolors." *Ka-thunk.* "Squirt gun." *Ka-thunk.* "Cup." *Klink.*

"What's all that for?" I wiggled my shoulders to adjust the weight.

"More colors. Not even in Darla's coloring books will you see a goat as swirly colorful as Morton's 'bout to be."

I wondered how many colors we'd turn by the time Mary Jane finished with us. "You've got to be three bats short in the hayloft. She'll flip."

"If that means I'm a genius, I know. But let's be fair. It was your idea."

"No, it wasn't. My idea was to turn *you* into a purple head with orange eyebrows. *You* turned the trick into a goat."

Bash bowed. "Thank you, thank you."

"I didn't mean it in a good way." I bounced my back. "You didn't forget to put the gross green back in the pack, did you? It's my favorite. It glows in the dark."

"Ha! I knew you cared."

"I just meant . . . Never mind. Let's just get this over with. Did you tell your mom we were going to Mary Jane's?"

"Yep. She said okay because Mary Jane's folks are there."

"Did you tell her why we're going?"

"To play with Morton."

My stomach hurt. We each wheeled a bicycle out of the garage, strapped on helmets, coasted down the driveway, and angled right onto the side of the road. We pedaled toward Morris's Corner Store and Seed Emporium. Bash shot past me. "This way." With a burst, he cut right, yanked up on the handlebars, and jumped the ditch.

I skidded to a halt and almost flopped down the bank face-first into the trickle of yucky drain water.

"You gotta pedal a million miles an hour, not slam on the brakes," Bash hooted.

"You gave me the slow bike."

I wheeled the bike down the bank, hopped the dirty water and walked the bike up the other side of the ditch. "The book bag's too heavy," I said.

"Yeah, right."

Bash pumped alongside the border of a hayfield and the edge of Morrises' side yard. I followed. Once we made it to the backyard, we turned left, and pedaled to the goat pasture. We leaned our bikes against fence posts. Bash peeked around. "Quiet now. We don't want Mary Jane catching us and spoiling the surprise."

I shuddered. "We don't want Mary Jane catching us. Period."

A door slammed. Bash flapped his arms. "Get down, get down. Here she comes."

We dropped, each of us behind a fence post. Mary Jane skipped out the back door of the Morrises' house, which made up the back half of their general store. She held a blue cloth bag. She flipped the latch on the gate to Morton's pasture. A white goat with a chocolate brown head and floppy ears popped up from a platform fastened into a shade tree and scampered down one of the old branches propped against the trunk—monkey bars for a goat. *"Maaa-haa-haa-haa-haaa."*

The goat leaped the last few feet and trotted toward Mary Jane. She bent toward him and scratched the goat between a set of horns that curled backward and ended in points. "There's my good boy. What a good boy. How's my Morty-Morton-Orton?"

Bash smooshed his face into the grass to stop from laughing. I clamped a hand over my mouth. *Morty-Morton-Orton?*

While holding the blue bag away from Morton, with her other hand, Mary Jane pulled some pellets from her pocket. "Here's some foody-oody-foody for you, Morty-Orty-Morton-Orton-Mortykins. Such a good boy."

I barely caught a glimpse of Morton nibbling pellets from Mary Jane's palm because now I had to smoosh my face into the dirt to smother my giggles. Mary Jane Morris the Proper baby-talks to goats? Awesome.

By the time Bash and I dared look up again, Mary Jane knelt at a giant tree stump in the center of the goat pasture that Morton used for playing king goat on the mountain. Morton nuzzled his little nose under Mary Jane's arm.

"Okay, first Morty-Orty, let's make sure nobody's peeking." She scanned the pasture.

"The bikes," I mouthed at Bash.

He shook his head, meaning, "Maybe she won't see them."

She did. Laser blue eyes locked onto the bikes, then burned across the field until they ferreted out Bash and, finally, me. She bellowed. "I see you spying on me! You come here this instant, Sebastian Nicholas Hinglehobb and Raymond William Boxby."

"What, no Bashy-Washy-Super-Pizzazzy?" Bash answered in a singsong voice. "Coming, Mary Janey-Laney-Fruity-Okayey."

Mary Jane stiffened. The hand not holding the blue pouch clenched. It gave Bash the second he needed to whisper instructions. "Ditch the book bag." While Bash stood, I wriggled out of the straps and scooted the pack into a clump of taller grass.

We climbed the fence. Morton galloped toward Bash. *"Maaa-haa-haa-haa-haaa."*

Bash dropped to a football stance and bleated back. *"Maaa-haa-haa-haa yourself."*

Bash lowered his head. Morton lowered his. They both charged.

This was not going to be good.

At the last second, Bash rolled out of the way, grabbed Morton around the shoulders, and they tumbled into a bleating heap. Morton licked Bash's nose. Bash chucked the goat's chin. Big, brown floppy ears snapped against the faces of both goat and boy as Morton shook his head.

Mary Jane stood, arms crossed, pointy-toed cowboy boot tapping. "How many times have I told you to stop playing the head-butting game?"

"I didn't. I played the avoid-the-head-butting game." Bash rubbed the goat's belly. Morton chewed on Bash's shirt. "Morty-Forty-Snorty-Orty's too big now."

Mary Jane flinched. "You taught *Morton* that when he was a kid."

"Morty-Cordy-Snorty-Martin-Orty's head was smaller then. An' not as hard." Bash and Morton nuzzled noses.

"Morton grew up, unlike some people I know."

Bash separated himself from the goat. "Mary Jane thinks it's my fault that Morton likes ramming into people."

Mary Jane stamped her pointy-toed cowboy boot. "It *is* your fault. You are the one who taught him that game."

"Nope. Goat kids already know. That's how they play." Bash patted Morton's shoulder. Morton chewed on Bash's pants pocket. "You only had Morton. So I played the other goat."

"Morton is not a kid anymore. He's a full-grown Boer show goat, and a very pretty one too. But now he thinks it's fine to charge into people because you, Sebastian Nicholas Hinglehobb, taught him that's what people do."

"Only when they're crouched in the football lineman stance. That's how we played."

I couldn't stand it any longer. "So what's in the bag?"

For a second, Mary Jane stared at the blue cloth pouch like it was a snake. Suddenly, she hid it behind her back and scanned the area all around the pasture. "Is anybody else hiding out there?"

Bash gave the pasture the once-over. "Nope. Just usy-kins."

"Okay, now listen up, you can't tell anybody. Ever since that robber began holding up businesses, we've taken precautions." Mary Jane knelt in front of the big stump again. "Whenever we get too much money in the cash register, we hide it until bank time, when Dad and Mom count it and get it ready for deposit."

She tugged a rock away from between two roots to reveal a hole at the bottom of the stump. "There's a hollow spot inside this oak." Her arm disappeared up to her shoulder inside the stump. When she pulled her arm out, her hand no longer held the bag. Mary Jane rolled the rock back into place, stood, and cowboy-boot-kicked the rock hard against the stump. "We figured the robber wouldn't think to look in the pasture."

Bash flashed a thumbs-up. "Excellent."

Mary Jane swung a pointy-toed cowboy boot. "That bag better be there when I come back for it after the store closes."

"'Course it will, Mary Jane. We came to play with Morton, not a crummy old bag."

Mary Jane narrowed her eyes at Bash, then at me. "I need to get back into the store with Dad. Don't teach Morton any more head-butting games."

"Nope, we won't. Bye, Mary Jane. The milk truck comes at four. Happy April Fool's Day."

Mary Jane squinted at both of us, stamped on the rock one more time, kissed Morton on the nose, and turned for the store. "Don't forget to close the gate."

We watched as she slammed her way through the back door. I blew out a long breath. "We better not do this. She's pretty grouchy."

"All the more reason to decorate the goat. MJ's awfully worried about her folks and the store. She needs a laugh. This'll do it."

"I don't think so."

"'Course it will. Why do you think I wanted to get her goat? To cheer her up. Grab the backpack. I'm gonna take Morty-Orty-Porty-Sorty-Gorty behind the tree so he's out of sight from Morrises' windows."

"Okay, but I get to spray the glow-in-the-dark gross green. It's my favorite."

"See? You do *too* wanna do this too."

"It's just that . . . Oh, forget it." I climbed the fence, pulled the book bag out of hiding, and hustled it behind the tree. Bash reached into his pocket and held out his hand.

"How come you carry goat pellets?"

"Tin cans take up too much room."

"Oh."

Morton nibbled pellets from Bash's hand. Bash dug into his pocket again and handed pellets to me. "Here, you feed. I'll paint."

"Save me some. The green. And the purple. I want to do the purple too."

Morton's soft, whiskery goat lips tickled as he munched pellets from my palm.

Bash sprayed lines, squiggles, and smiley faces all over the wiry hair of Morton's flank. He squirted the watercolors with his orange-tipped black squirt gun and brushed a picture of his riding hog, Gulliver J. McFrederick the Third, on Morton's back. He tried to paint Mary Jane's face on Morton's belly, but it looked more like a monkey. Or maybe he was trying to paint a monkey, and it looked a bit like Mary Jane. He used his farmer pocketknife to shave the chalk into cups, squirted the chalk dust, mixed it, and painted triangles, squares, swirlies, and circles.

Morton's once-white right side dripped in reds, greens, blues, yellows, pinks, purples, oranges, and a few colors I didn't know.

"Your turn." Bash handed me the book bag and took Morton.

I pulled out the can of glow-in-the-dark gross green. I stared at the white left on the goat. At the green can. Over my shoulder at Morrises' store. It was just for fun, right? To cheer up Mary Jane, right? She'll laugh. Won't she?

I held the can in the air and pushed the nozzle. *Sssst.* Green molecules floated in the breeze.

Bash tapped heads with Morton. "Hurry up, Beams."

I held my breath, aimed at the goat, and pressed. *Sssst.* It looked like a lime. I could do better. I took the squirt gun. *Shoop, shoop.* When the squirt gun ran out of water, I poured the chalk water into the gun and squirted that. Morton watched as I worked an ocean scene onto his belly, with a shark jumping out of the water to snatch a seagull flying over the goat's shoulder.

When I finished, Bash picked up the can of hurt-your-eyes-blue and sprayed "Happy April Fool's Day" down Morton's spine. "Now we gotta run him around real fast so the paint dries."

Thirty minutes later, we were back on our bicycles, pedaling back to the farm as fast as we could, laughing all the way.

"The blech-pink-and-snot-orange turtle on the gross-green surfboard's awesome, Beamer. You're an artist."

"Even Mary Jane has to like your purple polka-dotted rabbit with fire-red glasses and school-bus-yellow boots. And the purplish-orange and grayish-throw-up eyes all over Morton's legs was great." I pedaled harder. "She will like it, won't she?"

"'Course. Am I ever wrong?"

Uh-oh.

Chapter 13

Great Gallons of Chocolate Milk

The rumble of a big diesel engine rattled my ears. Monkey Man Bash let go of the limb of an apple tree and dropped to the orchard ground. "Hear that, Beamer?"

My stomach clenched. My heart scrambled up my throat. My brain screamed.

The milk truck.

Bash clapped bark from his hands. "This is gonna be such awesome-sauce. Let's go." He shot across the field.

I shuffled across the field toward the milking parlor. Would the milkman go spastic? What does 448 gallons of chocolate milk look like, anyway? My mouth twitched. I drooled at the thought of so much chocolate. It wouldn't hurt to guzzle a glass or two before getting grounded. I lowered my head and churned my legs like a bull charging the barn.

Whumpf. I splatted horns first—or would have if I had horns—into a galloping Jig.

"*Oof.*"

"*Ow.*"

Ka-plang.

We tumbled in a tangled mess into a parked bicycle. All three of us—Jig, bike, and me—rolled to a stop in front of tennis shoe toes. I looked up. Two flame-orange ponytails swished above me as Jag looked down, shaking her head. She snorted. "Boys. Always running, never looking."

Jig unclamped his teeth from the back tire. "Bonkers is here. We found his bicycle."

I tugged a leg from under Jig's armpit and unwedged my knee from the bike frame. "Yeah. I noticed."

Jig kicked his legs, bouncing the bicycle off both of us. "As soon as the milk truck left our place, we took off running for here."

Jag snorted again. "But some of us watched where we were going."

I scratched gravel from my palms and groaned my way to my feet. "We better get in there."

The three of us ran into the dairy barn and blasted our way through the door to the bulk tank room. A dark giant leaning over the tank jumped. Something clattered from one of his big, brown hands as he dove to the floor. "*Yipes.* More of them!"

I ducked. More what? Spiders? I looked around. I only saw Bash, Bonkers, Lauren, and Mary Jane. Heard only the refrigerator hum of the milk tank.

Bash winked. "Mr. Sneedlehouser was about to measure the milk. He's the milk truck driver." He leaned past the tank. "C'mon out, Mr. Sneedlehouser. It's just Jig and Jag, and Ray-Ray Sunbeam Beamer."

"Stop calling me that."

The shaking giant peered over the tank. "So it is. Right." He took a single step. "Is, uh, anyone else going to come crashing through that door?"

"Nope. We're all here."

The milkman hunched shoulders as bulky as feed sacks. Muscles quivered through his shirt sleeves. The door didn't move. So he reached again for the top of the bulk cooling tank. The milkman didn't need a stool. He pinched a handle, and started pulling a silver stick out of the tank.

I raised my hand. "What's that thing, Mr. Sneedlehouser? The way you dropped it when I came in, I thought it was a spider."

The milkman jumped. "Where?" The stick again clattered back into its slot.

Bash pushed his stool toward the tank. "No spiders, Mr. S. Pops doesn't allow 'em in here."

Mr. Sneedlehouser took off his baseball cap and scratched curly, black hair. He narrowed brown eyes at us. "Say, how come all you kids are here?"

From atop his stool, Bash swept a hand at us. "My cousin's a city kid, and Lauren's from Florida. You can show 'em how this stuff works."

Lauren kicked the stool. "There are more cows in Florida than Ohio, Pig Boy."

"But you never worked on a farm."

"Your dad hires me to help sometimes. Girls work better than boys, you know."

"I can outwork you any day of the week, Florida Girl."

Mr. Sneedlehouser backed against the wall. Mary Jane slipped between Lauren and Bash. "Sebastian Nicholas Hinglehobb. Lauren Michelle Rodriguez. We are not gathered here to prove that girls are better workers than boys. We already know that. We're here because of . . ." She leaned forward and whispered, ". . . the milk."

Bonkers snickered. Jag snorted. Lauren spun on one foot and marched away. "Fine. But Florida still has more cows than Ohio."

Mary Jane reached up and clutched Bash's arm. "And afterward, we shall discuss the color of goats." Her laser-blue eyes flashed my direction. "You too."

I gulped. Can a kid stow away on a milk truck if his life's in danger?

Bash grinned. "I hear goats come in many colors these days. Especially the first of April."

Mary Jane stamped a pointy-toed cowboy boot. "We. Shall. Talk." After a five-second stare-down, she turned to the milkman. "I'm sorry, Mr. Sneedlehouser. You can come out now. Pretend you're a teacher and it's career day."

The milkman's eyes darted between us and the cooling

tank. He pushed away from the wall. "Always wanted to be a teacher. I like teaching. It's the kids that make me nervous."

Mr. Sneedlehouser sized up his classroom. "Well, okay then, let's start. The first thing I did when I walked in here was this." He flicked a switch on the tank control panel. The humming of the tank grew louder. "I turned it off." He clicked again. The humming quietened.

"That's the agitator," Bash said.

I looked at the only agitator I knew square in his blue eyes. "The what?"

Mr. Sneedlehouser cleared his throat. Mary Jane crossed her arms. "Go ahead, Mr. Sneedlehouser. Some of us know we must keep our mouths shut to learn."

"That's why she doesn't know anything," Bash mumbled.

Mary Jane stomped a boot. Lauren stepped between her and Bash's stool. "Children, please." She looked over her shoulder and grinned at me.

Mr. Sneedlehouser shuffled. "Yes, well, anyway . . ." He pointed behind us where a big, clear hose poked through an opening high on the block wall and ran to the bulk tank. "The milk is pumped from the parlor through that cooling hose into this insulated, refrigerated tank."

Mr. Sneedlehouser pointed to the middle of the top of the tank. "The agitator is a stainless steel rod with paddles that constantly stirs the milk inside the cooling tank."

Bonkers leaned toward my ear. "Or it's like a big spoon stirring a giant glass of chocolate milk."

Mary Jane raised her hand. "Stirring keeps the milk at a consistent temperature all the way through, not just on the sides where the refrigeration is."

Mr. Sneedlehouser smiled at Mary Jane. "That's right. And it keeps all the cream from rising to the top and forming in a thick layer."

Bash hopped off the stool and pushed past Mary Jane. "So now you're going to pump the milk into your truck, right? Let me hook up the hose."

"First, I need to measure how much milk is in the tank. So I turn off the agitator, and open the lid." Mr. Sneedlehouser again flipped back a cap on top of the tank, and this time pulled the longest dipstick I'd ever seen out of the tank. "These notches on the measuring stick indicate pounds . . ."

The milkman froze. A frothy brown liquid ran down the flat surface of the stainless steel stick. He threw back the big lid to the tank and peered inside. And kept staring. "How in the world . . . Oh, this will never . . . How am I going to explain . . ."

His eyebrows rode up his forehead, like fuzzy bulldozers pushing a pile of wrinkles. In a very small voice, he said to Bash, "You better get your dad."

Bash grinned. "Somethin' wrong?"

"Just get your dad."

"Sure thing."

Mr. Sneedlehouser backed away from the tank. A couple minutes later, Bash crashed through the door, followed by Uncle Rollie and Aunt Tillie holding Darla.

Uncle Rollie tapped his hat brim. "Afternoon, Dave, and how are you, no doubt?"

The milkman's eyes never left the tank. "Rollie. Look. In. The. Tank."

Uncle Rollie's brow arched. He stepped onto a stool and squinted down the hatch. His eyes narrowed.

Aunt Tillie's eyelid ticked. "What is it, Roland?"

Uncle Rollie slid the dipstick out. Brown broth dripped into his palm. He sniffed it. Slurped it. And smacked his lips. "Offhand, I'd say it's chocolate milk. Dave, dip that sample cup in there."

"Chocolate . . . milk?" Aunt Tillie's eye tic picked up pace. She lowered Darla to the floor and seemed to notice the rest of us for the first time. "Chocolate milk *and* a barn full of kids."

The milk truck driver dipped a small steel cup on a long handle into the cooling tank. He pulled out the cup, squinted, and shook it into a swirl. A couple brown drops sloshed over the brim.

The driver put the cup to his lips and drank. "Chocolate milk. How did your cows . . . ?"

Bash muffled a snicker into the back of my T-shirt. Lauren and Jag held each other. Jig ran laps around Bash and me. Darla followed him, squealing, "Choco milk. Choco milk!" Bonkers edged toward the door.

Mary Jane, her words melting like chocolate candy in the sun, smiled sweetly. "Is something the matter, Mr. Hinglehobb?"

Uncle Rollie's blue eyes narrowed beneath furry eyebrows. He spoke so quietly, I had to strain my ears to hear him: "I'd reckon I'd raised the first cows to milk chocolate, Dave, except for one thing." He tapped the Hoard's Dairyman calendar on the wall.

Mr. Sneedlehouser downed the rest of the chocolate milk and dropped the dip cup into the sterilization sink. "It's April. So?"

"April first." Uncle Rollie looked over my shoulder at the thing snickering into my back. "Right, Sebastian?"

The Basher stepped into the spotlight. "Hey, Pops, you know where chocolate milk comes from? Brown cows."

Uncle Rollie wasn't laughing. "We don't have brown cows." I ducked behind Bash.

"Must be a roving herd of Brown Swiss cows that sneaked into the barn, huh, Pops?"

Aunt Tillie set an eye tic speed record as she peered into the tank. I thought I saw steam curling from Uncle Rollie's ear hair.

Mary Jane glanced at the door. She'd have to run over Bonkers to get to it. Lauren, Jig, and Jag angled toward the windows. I debated between door and windows.

Bash snickered. "Brown Swiss chocolate milk. Pretty cool, huh, Pops?"

Uncle Rollie crossed tree trunk arms across his barrel chest and squinted at Bash. "Do you have any idea how many gallons of milk you just ruined?"

"It's not ruined, Pops. It's better. It's chocolate."

"It's contaminated." Mr. Sneedlehouser took a clipboard from the wall, and scratched lines through the top sheet. "The whole batch has to be dumped."

"Horse feathers." Uncle Rollie's face reddened. "An entire day's milk production wasted. A full day's milk pay gone." His forehead furrowed so harshly that his eyebrows looked like a caterpillar quivering at the top of his eyeballs.

"Where'd you learn that such tomfoolery was acceptable behavior?"

Bash's smile vanished. "It's not tomfoolery. It's April Foolery." He shrank backward.

"Stay right where you are. All of you." Uncle Rollie closed his eyes. The caterpillar eyebrows bulged.

Aunt Tillie, her eye no longer ticking, took Uncle Rollie's arm. "Roland, Tom had nothing to do with this foolery. You know very well where your son learned his April Foolery."

A muscle in Uncle Rollie's neck twitched. His jaw clenched. "The boy hasn't got the sense he was born with. How in the world . . ." The words trailed off.

Aunt Tillie squeezed his hand. He glowered. With her free hand, she pointed to her forehead. Her finger trailed to her check, decorated with a black-smudged heart. "I believe the boy learned plenty from a very enthusiastic teacher."

Uncle Rollie's eyes locked onto Aunt Tillie's cheek. "But not this . . ." His teeth ground. "Mattie, the boy can't . . ." He daubed at the heart tattoo and studied the smudge it left on his fingertip.

His jaw relaxed. Uncle Rollie blew about thirty seconds of air through his mustache. Finally, he spoke softly to Aunt Tillie. "Okay, it wasn't Tom who taught him. Who's April?"

Aunt Tillie quirked a grin. "Edna's sister, I believe. Edna Foolery."

Suddenly, Uncle Rollie burst into an explosion of laughter. "Champ, you beat me at my own game." He clapped Bash on the shoulder. "A game we aren't going to play anymore. Right?"

"Right, Pops." Bash wiped a trickle of sweat from his forehead.

The milkman patted the tank. "Say, do you have a glass around here? Before we dump it, I wouldn't mind another drink."

Bash ran to the sink, grabbed a cup, and wiped it out with the bottom of his T-shirt. "Here ya go, Mr. S. Chocolate milk's the best. Good thing the cows gave it today, huh? We'd drink it all ourselves if we could."

Uncle Rollie doffed his cap and scratched the bald part of his head. "Oh, I believe you will. How many gallons do we have there, Dave?"

Mr. Sneedlehouser slid the measuring stick out of the tank and squinted at the lines and numbers etched on the surface. "Looks to be about 3,625 pounds. So that would be . . ." He tapped a calculator.

I sighed. "453 gallons."

Mr. Sneedlehouser looked up from his calculator. ". . . 453 gallons. And five ounces."

Uncle Rollie stroked his mustache. "A good milk day. That's a lot of drinking. Ray?"

I gulped. "That's 3,624 glasses of milk."

"And five ounces," Mr. Sneedlehouser said.

Uncle Rollie nodded. "And I count seven of you in on it, so . . . ?"

I tried running the numbers in my head. "I'm not so hot with division."

The milkman tapped his calculator keys. "Comes out to just about 518 glasses of milk each. Before the milk spoils."

Uncle Rollie folded his arms, crossed his legs at the ankles, and leaned against the big, steel tank. "Well then, you kids better start rounding up all the clean containers you can. Gallon jugs. Five-gallon pails. Antique eight-gallon milk cans your moms might be using for decoration. You've got an awful lot of chocolate milk to drink, and I need this cooler empty and sterilized by evening milking."

We stared at him. Where were we going to find that many empty bottles?

Uncle Rollie pulled a cell phone from his pocket. "I'd start now if I were you. I'll just be calling all your folks to let them know you're coming. Oh, and Bash . . ."

"Um, yeah, Pops?"

"I believe you've just lost your allowance for a full year. Let's call it your milk money."

Bash gulped. "Yes, Pops."

"So when did that, uh, herd of Brown Swiss pull off this prank?"

"They got up awfully early in the morning, Pops. Awfully early."

Chapter 14

Owls, Oaks, and Uh-Oh

I sloshed to the end of the driveway, where Lauren, Mary Jane, and Jag swayed like sick pelicans on the big rock. I held my belly. "I don't feel so good."

Lauren whimpered. "I never drank so much chocolate milk in my life."

Mary Jane groaned. "Every time I emptied my glass last night, Mom refilled it. She even poured chocolate milk on my oatmeal this morning."

Jag snorted. "I think my mom baked chocolate milk in the meatloaf."

I lowered myself to the grass. "I don't think our chocolate milk joke went over too well."

"I think the joke's still going," Lauren said. "And it's on us."

"Where's Jig?" I asked.

Jag snorted again. "He said he wasn't running with a bunch of girls."

"Christopher Joseph Dennison said he was too sick to run when I called him. I think it's the chocolate milk." Mary Jane threaded her hair into a pink scrunchie. "Where is Sebastian Nicholas Hinglehobb, that goat-coloring rat?"

"Taking a nap. He said he already outruns all of us."

Jag snorted. "Bash doesn't take naps."

Mary Jane grunted. "He'd better not be napping tomorrow. You and he have a goat to scrub. See to it, Raymond William Boxby."

I flopped onto my back and rubbed my bulging belly. "Let's not run today."

Lauren moaned to her feet. Her yellow jersey with the blue and white number nine strained a little across her belly. "I can't break training. I'm not letting you break yours either."

Mary Jane dusted her all-pink running outfit. "I picked a fine morning to join you."

Jag tugged at her too-long gym shorts—red today—and straightened her play dress—orange and yellow polka dots.

I rolled to my knees and worked my way up. "All right. But don't go too fast."

"Not today I won't," Lauren said. "Stretch a little first."

Stretch? My calves ached from the run two days ago. I barely made it clunking down the stairs this morning. Video games never hurt like this.

"Running is so much better than sitting on a couch playing video games." Mary Jane touched her toes. "Running's my favorite part about volleyball season, after spiking the ball. And blocking the other team's spikes. Video games turn you into a boring blob."

I touched my knees and winced. "Boring blob's not so bad once you get used to it."

"You've never spiked a volleyball, have you?"

Jag snorted. "You can't hang upside down from real trees in a video game."

Lauren hopped around doing a jumping-jack sort of thing. "Or outrun a fly ball. That's totally cool when the softball smacks into your mitt."

"I once hit thirty-seven home runs in a row on my Super Vid Power Player baseball game."

The girls stared at each other. Lauren's cheeks puffed. Mary Jane's nose flared. Jag's flame-colored eyebrows jiggled on her freckled forehead. All three bubbling girl bombs exploded in giggles. They shook from hair scrunchies to pink kitty running shoe laces. Laughing seemed to be the only time Jag didn't snort. She honked.

I didn't see what was so funny. Not a thing, really. But a snicker ran up my belly, tickled my throat, and jumped out with a snort. I tried to choke back a *hee hee,* but the *snerk, snerk, snork* spilled right out. I couldn't help it. Maybe it was Jag's honking. Lauren's giggle. Mary Jane's guffaws. Laughing's a disease, and I caught it.

Lauren finally braced herself against the big rock. "Thanks, Raymond. Best stretching exercise ever. It was a milkshake. Some of the chocolate milk shook right out."

Mary Jane sighed. "That was wonderful. I'm ready to go."

Jag's honk returned to a snort.

I stopped laughing too. They never did tell me what was so funny. I didn't want to ask. I ached too much for them to start the giggle disease again.

Lauren ran in place, kicking her knees nearly to her chin. "Today will be a pretty easy run. We're going to take the trail through the woods."

I gulped. "I don't think so. What if the robber's there?"

"Robbers hide in hideouts, not in woods." Lauren jogged to the side of the road. "And the trail is pretty."

"Right behind you, Lauren Michelle Rodriguez." Mary Jane loped into line.

Jag snorted and ran beside Mary Jane.

I thought about sneaking back to the house. If I did, someone would force another cup of chocolate milk on me. The woods, or chocolate milk? I lumbered to the roadside.

"What a beautiful morning for a run," Lauren gushed after two minutes or so of what she called *easy* running.

"Magnificent," Mary Jane said.

"Sweet," Jag said.

"*Uffa, uffa.*" I couldn't talk. My belly said enough for both of us: *Splish. Splosh. Splish. Splosh.* How'd I drink that much chocolate milk?

We ran past Uncle Rollie's hayfield to the edge of the woods. Lauren waved. "There's the trail." She jumped the ditch, and padded into the woods. Mary Jane leaped the ditch and trotted after her. Jag flew across the gap and honked after them.

I stumbled down the ditch, splashed through the drainage

water, clawed my way back up, and ran into the woods. "Wai . . . *uffa* . . . for . . . *uffa, uffa* . . . me . . . *effaaaaa*."

We wound along a deer trail—the deer left droppings that I tried to hop over—through cool shadows and dashes of sunlight. The beginnings of a bright green new leaves from spring muffled road and tractor sounds. Birds tweeted, rapped, and chirped songs. It was like having fifteen quiet radios on at once, all tuned to different stations.

The girls slowed their pace to gawk at blue, yellow, and orange wildflowers. Chipmunks *nyuk, nyuk, nyuked* and scampered under clusters of small, leafy bushes. Squirrels *uhuhuh-ink, uhuhuh-inked* as they leaped from tree branch to wavy tree branch.

Lauren put on the brakes and threw up her hand. Mary Jane and Jag stopped, and I trotted up to them. "What's—"

Lauren pointed into the woods. Hunkered on a branch about two trees away, a brown-and-white-speckled owl with a big white face and a tiny beak like a pale yellow baby carrot studied us.

"Beautiful," Mary Jane whispered.

Jag twirled one of her two fiery ponytails. "Wow, wow, wow."

I poked at my glasses. "I thought owls only came out at night."

The owl blinked big, black marble eyes. Mary Jane gave the tiniest shake of her head. "That's a barred owl. Sometimes you hear them during the day too."

Lauren inched closer to Mary Jane. "What do they sound like?"

"They make lots of sounds. I know this one." Mary Jane closed her eyes for a second. She leaned a tad toward the owl, and cooed: *Who cooks for you? Who cooks for you?*"

The owl's head turned slightly. Its chest feathers puffed. In a voice that almost sounded like a whispering dog woofing, it called: *"Ooh-ooh-oo-ooh, ooh-ooh-oo-oooooh."*

Lauren giggled. "It kinda does sound like 'Who cooks for you.'"

We watched the owl. The owl watched us. Mary Jane put her hand on Lauren's shoulder. "We better keep going."

Lauren sighed. She turned and shuffled along the dirt trail. I could keep up with this pace.

Ragged branches dripped from lopsided trees. Funky-looking gray rocks poked out of the ground in odd places. Scraggly strands of weeds and fuzzy clumps of moss littered the ground, along with leaves, twigs, dirt, pebbles, and animal droppings. It was a whole bunch of all the things that moms hate having tracked into the house, but scattered all together, they added up to the prettiest place I'd ever seen. Maybe there's no such thing as ugly. All mixed together, ugly looks pretty awesome.

A brown rabbit sprang across the winding trail. We hopped a log. Twigs cracked under our feet. Leaves whooshed through our hair. We squished over moss and splashed through a stream.

We ran upon a fallen tree beside the trail. Lauren scrambled along the upturned rooted end and balanced her way across the trunk. Mary Jane, Jag, and I followed on the barked balancing beam. Lauren hopped off and swung back onto the trail. We followed the leader.

I listened to chatter and chirping. Breezes rustled leaves and cooled my face. The woods smelled a bit like wet dog mixed with flower shop scents. It was awesome.

I swept my hands around me. "How did God think up all this stuff?"

"Because He's God," Mary Jane said.

"But look at all of this. It's awesome. *Awe. Some.*"

Lauren picked up an acorn. "But He doesn't just say *poof* once a week, and there's another tall tree." She bounced the acorn in her palm. "See that big oak tree over there." She held the acorn up to her eye. "It grew from a tiny acorn just like this."

Jag snorted. "It was a nut, just like you."

Lauren tossed the acorn into the woods. "That will be a tree. Unless the squirrels eat it. Then it will be food to make them grow."

I rubbed my chin. "Bonkers, Bash, and I found tadpoles in the creek. They told me those squiggly blobs would become frogs. I thought they were crazy. But we have tiny, blobby frogs in the fish tank on Bash's desk. They're Transformers."

Lauren nodded. "Maybe that's what baptism is about. You go in the water a tadpole and come out a beautiful frog."

Mary Jane grimaced. "I'm not a frog."

I bit my tongue. There's a time to speak, and there's a time to not get slugged.

Lauren leaned forward. "You were baptized? What happened?"

Mary Jane slid the pink scrunchie out of her hair and shook her chocolate-brown curls. "After I asked Jesus to forgive me of my sins, all those things I did that were wrong, and promised to not do them anymore with His help, Jesus filled my heart. That was when I, uh, changed from a tadpole to a frog."

I poked my glasses back into place. "So what's the water for?"

Mary Jane put the scrunchie back in her hair. I wish she'd make up her mind. "Pastor Randy said it showed our commitment. And it's in the Bible."

"But why?"

Lauren wiped the back of her hand across her brow. "I can look up some stuff up in the Farmin' and Fishin' Book during my prayer time today. You can, too, Raymond. Let's see what we—"

Jag tugged at Lauren's shirt. "Whose footprints are those?"

We tiptoed over to a muddy spot just off the trail. Big, deep shoe prints showed in the ooze. The long part of the foot looked wide and smooth. The heel part showed some kind of tiny design in the middle.

I showed the bottom side of my sneaker. Smaller, with lots of diamond-shaped hashes. Mary Jane showed hers. Swirly patterns, and too small. Lauren shook her head. She and Jag both wore shoes skinnier and tinier than those footprints. I'd never seen Bash, Bonkers, nor Jig wear smooth shoes anywhere near that size. Uncle Rollie wore work boots with lots of traction marks. Mr. Dennison on the other side of the woods wore work boots too.

I stiffened. "The robber. You said robbers hide in hideouts, not woods."

"Maybe he has a tent out here." Lauren bit her lip. "I think we found a clue."

Mary Jane backed up. "The footprints go that way, ahead. I think we should very, very quietly walk back the way we came."

I was already running. Lauren passed me, but I stayed ahead of Mary Jane and Jag. At least I hoped it was their feet I heard right behind me.

"Move, Raymond."

Mary Jane slipped past. I kicked it up another gear. I overtook her and was gaining on Lauren when we crashed through the opening to the woods and jumped the ditch. A horrible cramp crushed my side like a giant bear paw squeezing my ribs. I didn't care. Lauren, Mary Jane, Jag, and I never stopped till we got back to the farm. Well, that's where I stopped. The girls kept running toward Mary Jane's store. I sure didn't want to be close to any store, not with a robber in the woods.

Oh no. I just remembered. We have to go the store tomorrow to wash a goat.

Chapter 15

Hunting Bears and Praying for a Mantis

I squinted down the orange barrel, lined up the blue sights, and squeezed the yellow trigger. *Sproing.*

Pfft. A foam dart bounced off Bash's closet door, left and low of the circle target hanging there.

"Your dart gun shoots crooked, Bash."

Bash hooted. "It's not the gun."

"Then it's the chocolate milk. I've never been allowed to drink that much chocolate milk at once before." I rubbed my belly and groaned. "Never has a grown-up ordered me to drink more chocolate before I could be excused from the dinner table."

"Supper," Bash said. But he grimaced too.

A long, green creepy-looking praying mantis perched on the edge of the pollywog tank and stared at me. "What's that bug doing?"

"Probably laughing. You shoot funny."

Black blobbies with little legs squiggled in the water, while tan spotted critters that looked kind of like frogs with tiny tails clung to rocks, leaves, and branches at one end of the tank. Their sides shook too. "It's the gun," I yelled at the laughing froglets.

"C'mon, try again. We gotta learn to protect ourselves." Bash tossed me another foam dart. "So you found a clue. Wanna go catch the robber?"

"We saw footprints in the woods. Could have been anybody."

"Who?"

"I don't know. Anybody."

"So it's the robber."

Crunk. I jammed another foam dart into the plastic gun. "I don't think we're going to scare a robber with a blue, orange, yellow, and red gun that looks like a plastic doughnut with a trigger." I aimed at the target. *Sproing. Pfft.* The foam dart bounced off the wall.

Bash tumbled backward on his bed and laughed. "When's the last time you cleaned your glasses? You even missed the door."

"Forget the foam darts. My plan is to run like crazy."

The mantis arched up a little taller and folded its front legs to its skinny chest. The little claw-like hands twitched. I was sure I heard tiny bug snickers through its beaky jaws. "What's that freaky bug doing in here anyway?"

"Probably wants to eat the tadpoles. Mantises are cool. The little ones eat flies and crickets, but the big mantises eat snakes, lizards, and frogs."

"He should try chocolate milk. I can't believe your dad sent two more glasses up to bed with us."

Bash jumped out of the bed and yanked open the closet door. "Keep practicin', Beams. I'm safe in here as long as it's where you're aiming."

"That's so funny I forgot to laugh," I muttered.

Bash burrowed into the boxes of junk on the floor of the closet. Things crashed, banged, and bounced. A frayed basketball bounced out and got stuck trying to roll under my bed. The noise stopped. "Hey, look what I found!"

Bash popped out of the closet and waved a green, black, and purple contraption. "It shoots water pellets. It's sorta like paintball, without the paint."

"Your mom will yell at us if you shoot water pellets in your room."

"It's not for the bedroom. We're goin' to hunt bears in the woods."

"You can't hunt bears with a water pellet gun."

"Why not?"

"There aren't any bullets."

"There aren't any bears."

I reached for another foam dart. "So why hunt them?"

"Because there aren't any. If there were, it would be stupid to use water pellets to hunt them."

I jammed the dart into the doughnut gun. "What I mean is, why hunt for what's not there?"

"If there were bears, I sure wouldn't want to find one. So I hunt for them when they're not there."

I scratched my head with the rubber suction tip of the loaded foam dart. "That doesn't make any sense."

"Sure it does. Lemme find the water pellets." Bash dove back into his closet. "You can take the dart gun."

"It doesn't shoot straight." The monster mantis leaned into the pollywog tank. I fired a foam dart. And yelped.

"Oh no! Bash!"

Bash scrambled out of the closet. "What?"

"I hit the praying mantis."

"Congratulations."

"No, no, no. I think I killed him. He's lying on the desk between the two glasses of chocolate milk."

Bash scooped up the big green bug. He stroked the long, broad wings with his fingertip. "It's not moving. What were you aiming at, the chair?"

"I aimed at the mantis. I didn't think I'd hit him." I grabbed my chest as another thought slapped me. "In my old school, a kid named Danny James told me once that some bugs are so rare that they're federally protected. I think the praying mantis was one."

"Cool."

"Not cool. I'm going to jail."

"Double cool."

"No, it's not." I looked around for hiding places. "We have to tell your mom."

Bash gently set the praying mantis on the windowsill. "Last I saw Ma, she was swatting flies. You want me to interrupt her fly-swattin' to tell her you killed a bug?"

"A federally protected bug. Oh, man, the FBI will be here any minute. Is prison like school? I don't think I'll like prison."

Bash pried the dart gun from my hand and tossed it on the bed. "You can hide out in our sugar shack. Pops won't need it again until next March when the sap starts runnin', and it's time to make maple syrup again."

I grabbed Bash by the shoulders. "I'm serious. And it was your gun. I bet they're going to arrest you too."

"If we both gotta hide out, we better hope Pops left a couple bottles of maple syrup in the sugar shack." He knocked my hands off his shoulders. "Chill out, Beamer. The FBI doesn't care about bugs."

"The sheriff, then. Is that a siren I hear? They're coming for me, aren't they? Tell Mom and Dad good-bye for me."

Bash bopped me with a pillow. "That was a cow. You're not going to make a very good hunter. That's why I only hunt for what isn't there. That's what happens when you aim at what is."

"You still don't make any sense." I sunk into the desk chair. "And I'm still doomed."

"You're a doofus. Take a look at the window."

I turned. Praying mantis legs quivered, found a hold on the sill, and pushed.

The mantis lived!

"He's not dead," I whispered.

The bug wobbled to his feet. He swayed for a few seconds.

"He's not dead," I repeated out loud.

The mantis arched its back and did a bug sit-up. He pulled his front legs up and folded them under his chin or whatever a bug mouth is called. It looked like he was thanking God.

I jumped up. "Cancel the FBI. The praying mantis isn't dead," I yelled.

The mantis spread his wings and tested them with a *hiss-zip* sound. The bug glared at me, turned, and flew away.

"Woo hoo!"

Bash shook his head. "Silly ol' bear." But he was grinning.

I plopped into the desk chair. "Let's ditch the dart guns."

"I only have one water pellet gun. You can use my squirt gun."

"No, no, we're not hunting a robber with dart guns, or water pellet guns, or squirt guns. We can't hunt him."

"Why not?"

"Because he's there."

Bash chewed on his tongue. "There is that."

I got up and unstuck the basketball wedged partly under the bed. "He's a robber. He holds up stores. And he has a real gun. A real gun, Bash, not these toys."

"He's never used it."

"He might. I don't want to be there if he does." I zinged the basketball underhanded at Bash. He caught it without taking his eyes off me. I shook my head. "We need something else."

Bash flopped onto his bed. He rolled onto his back and tossed the ball at the ceiling. It was a game we played whenever we were grounded—see how close we could come to hitting the ceiling without actually touching it. Bash's shot missed the ceiling by about the thickness of a sheet of notebook paper. We'd had a lot of practice.

Bash caught the ball just before it bopped his nose. "We could wait till he comes out, and tackle him with my kazoo and a birthday candle in a chocolate milk pitcher."

I stared at my goofball cousin. "Now that's just crazy."

Bash tossed the ball at the ceiling again. I flung my pillow to try to knock it out of the air. Missed. Bash caught the ball just before it mashed his nose. "No it's not. It's in the Farmin' and Fishin' Book."

Bash sat up and whipped the ball over his shoulder at me. It hit me in the nose. *"Ow."* While I still rubbed my nose, Bash returned my pillow. Fast. It whapped the back of my nose-rubbing hand. *"Ow.* You just made me punch myself."

I grabbed both ball and pillow. Bash flopped over and reached under the bed for his Bible. "There's an awesome story in here 'bout a bunch of guys who beat a big army with trumpets made out of sheep horns and torches in water pitchers they had to smash. An' they yelled a lot too."

I rolled onto my back. "You're making that up." I tossed the ball at the ceiling. *Broinnng.* Oops.

"No, really." Bash rifled pages. "Somewhere toward the front . . . Here it is. In the book of Judges, the story of Gideon."

"Was he nuts?" Tossed the ball. Just missed the ceiling. Caught it. *Phew.*

Bash scooped a couple dirty socks off the floor. "Nope. He talked to God."

"Better than talking to you." I tossed the basketball. Bash winged a ball of dirty socks. *Thwack.* He knocked the basketball out of the air. *Broinnng.* The basketball hit the wall. *Whump.* And landed on the bed next to my knee.

Bash pumped his fist. "*Ha.* Fastest dirty socks in the Midwest."

I picked up the pillow, thought about hurling it at Bash, and instead stuffed it under my head. "Okay, tell me the story. It'll keep you from bothering me while I try to figure a way out of this mess."

"Cool." History Teacher Bash wriggled on his bed until he sat against the wall, his Bible propped against tucked-up knees. "It starts here in chapter six. The people of Israel weren't doing what God told 'em to do, so God stepped back an' let a whole fleet of people called the Midians pick on 'em. Every time the Israel farmers' crops were ready for harvest, the Midians swarmed in with their cows and camels and ate everything. Then they'd take off with all of Israel's sheep, an' donkeys, an' oxen, an' stuff."

I reached for the basketball. "That was harsh."

"Yeah. So the Israel people started talkin' to God again, which is what God wanted in the first place. So God tells an Israel wheat farmer named Gideon that He's gonna use him to stomp the Midians. 'Cept God wanted to make it look impossible."

I spun the basketball in my hands. "That makes as much sense as you only hunting bears that aren't there."

History Teacher Bash marked his place with a finger and looked up. "Sure it does. God does all kinds of stuff for us when we let Him. But if it's too easy, we think we did it ourselves. So sometimes God makes sure there's no way we can do it alone."

That about summed it up. There was a robber running around, and all I had was an insane cousin who painted goats and loaded my slippers with shaving cream, a dart gun that didn't shoot straight, and more pitchers of chocolate milk than I cared to count. I couldn't think of anything much more impossible than that.

I stopped spinning the basketball. "Okay, let's hear the story of Gideon and how to stop a robber with candles, kazoos, and chocolate-milk pitchers."

Chapter 16

Candles, Kazoos, and Chocolate Milk Pitchers

History Teacher Bash flipped a page and traced words with his finger. "In chapter seven of Judges, Gideon gathers an army of 32,000 people in the mountain above the Midians' big ol' camp in the valley."

I tossed the basketball toward the ceiling. "That's a lot of people." The ball brushed the ceiling and dropped into my hands.

"Yeah, but there were a lot more Midians. And they had their friends with 'em. Verse twelve says they 'settled down in the valley like a swarm of locusts, and their camels were as innumerable as the sand on the seashore.'"

I spun the ball between my hands. "I grew up in Virginia Beach, remember. I've been to the seashore. That's like millions and millions of soldiers. Billions, maybe. Gideon's way outnumbered."

"Yeah, but listen to this." Bash pulled his Bible nearly to his nose. "'The LORD said to Gideon, "You have too many people for Me to hand the Midianites over to you, or else Israel might brag: 'I did it myself.' Now announce in the presence of the people: 'Whoever is fearful and trembling may turn back and leave Mount Gilead.' So 22,000 of the people turned back, but 10,000 remained.'""

I tossed the ball, softer this time. "Eek. So who'd God send to replace the fraidy-cats who ran away? Giants? Wolves? Ducks with sharp teeth?" The ball missed the ceiling. Then I missed the ball. It plunked onto my chest. *Umph.*

"Ducks don't have teeth. Listen to this part. It's awesome. It starts in verse four." Bash pulled the Bible in close again. "'Then the LORD said to Gideon, "There are still too many people."'"

"No way." I popped up like toast. The basketball fell and bounced across the floor. "I bet God sent bears. Really big ones."

"Nope." History Teacher Bash shook his head and kept reading: "'So he brought the people down to the water, and the LORD said to Gideon, "Separate everyone who laps water with his tongue like a dog. Do the same with everyone who kneels to drink." The number of those who lapped with their hands to their mouths was 300 men, and all the rest of the people knelt to drink water. The LORD said to Gideon, "I will deliver you with the 300 men who lapped and hand the Midianites over to you. But everyone else is to go home."'"

I held up my hand. "Why?"

"Watch." He set down his Bible, got onto all fours, and sunk his head into the bed.

"What are you doing?"

Bash looked up. "Drinking water."

"Not unless you wet the bed."

Bash spit. "Not that. I mean I'm acting it out. The ones God sent away got down like this, put their faces in the water and gulped it down. Now let me try the other way." Bash popped up to his knees, cupped his hands, and pretended to scoop water off the sheet.

I slung my pillow at Bash. "Are you sure you didn't wet the bed?"

"'Course not." Bash swatted the pillow away with cupped hands, then slurped imaginary water from his palms. *"Llup, llup, llup."* He made sure not to drip anything on the wet bed.

I rolled my eyes. "That's weird."

"Nope." Actor Bash dropped his hands, letting the rest of the imaginary water splash onto the imaginary bed. "I saw the pillow fast enough to knock it down." Bash snapped a corner of the pillow and sent it hurling back at me.

I peeled the pillow off my face. "So?"

"I see you. I see the pillow. But when I stick my head in the river"—Bash dropped back to all fours and smooshed his face into the bed—"my man't mee moo."

I smacked him on top of the head with the pillow. "What?"

Actor Bash looked up. "I can't see you. And I didn't see the pillow coming."

"So the guys who scooped water in their hands—"

Bash nodded. "Were always ready. Nobody could sneak up on them."

"But you can drink a lot more a lot faster if you get your face right down in there."

Bash scratched his ear. "Okay, maybe that's another point. The guys with too much water sloshed when they walked."

I groaned. "Yeah, none of us ran very well today with a million gallons of chocolate milk splashing around in our bellies." I slid out of bed, grabbed the basketball, and flopped backward onto the bed.

"So God only wanted to use people prepared to win. An' with the scaredy-cats and belly-sloshers sent home, that left only 300 water-lappers to face the millions of locusts. Just right for God."

I tossed the basketball. "So the water-lappers picked up everyone else's swords?"

"That's what I've been trying to tell you. They didn't use swords. Just kazoos, and birthday candles in chocolate-milk jars." Bash fished a pair of dirty socks off the floor and rolled them into a ball.

"Nuh-uh."

"Well, they used curly horns from rams. You poke a hole in the pointy end and blow through that, and it sounds like a weird trumpet kazoo."

"Neat. Do you have any rams?"

I tossed the basketball. Bash whizzed the sock roll at the basketball, pinging it halfway to the ceiling. The ball rolled down the wall and thunked to the bed, next to the sock roll. "Nope. A ram's a sheep. Closest thing around here is Mary Jane's buck. And Morton's still using his horns."

"Oh."

"The pitchers were water jars made of clay. An' they used torches, big ol' sticks like giant matches, but they burned longer."

I bounced the sock roll in my hand, then tossed it at the ceiling. Not even close. "We're not even allowed to play with birthday candles anymore, not after that last time."

Bash winced. "Lemme finish the story." History Teacher Actor Bash sat against the wall and picked up his Bible. "In verse sixteen, it says Gideon divided his 300 guys into three companies, an' gave every one a trumpet, an' an empty pitcher with a torch hidden inside. He set 'em up around the camp with all the locusts and camels."

"Why?" I threw the socks. Hit the ceiling.

"It's what God told him to do. Right about midnight, they attacked."

Threw the socks. "With giant candles and sheep horns?" Just missed. Perfect.

"Yeah. Here's what it says in verse nineteen: 'They blew their trumpets and broke the pitchers that were in their hands. The three companies blew their trumpets and shattered their pitchers. They held their torches in their left hands, their trumpets in their right hands, and shouted, "A sword for Yahweh and for Gideon!"'"

I tossed the socks. "Who's Yahweh?"

"God. That's His name. One of His names. Gideon wanted to make sure the people knew God did it."

The socks landed on my nose. I got a good whiff. *"Galaaaack.* That's gross! Do you even wash your feet?" I hacked a couple more times and hurled the sock ball at the closet. *"Phew-weee."* I shook my head. "Anyway, what happened?"

History Teacher Actor Bash grinned, but whether from the story or my wrinkled face, I wasn't sure. "What if you heard 300 dishes crashing to the ground all at once, and 300 lights snapping on, and 300 grown-ups yellin' all at once about sticks, or wooden spoons, or somethin'?"

I scratched my head. "I'd think you just got me into trouble again. And I'd run for it."

Bash drew a check mark in the air. "Score. The locust guys jumped up and started swinging their swords at anything that moved—which was only themselves."

"So they—?"

"Yep, they beat up each other. Gideon's guys stood there with ram kazoos in their right hands, and birthday candles in their left hands, and watched the bad guys fight the war all by themselves. The bad guys who were left got so scared that they ran away. That's when Gideon called in the rest of the Israelites to go chase 'em down."

I fell back against the wall. "Wow. So first God made it impossible for Gideon to win."

Bash closed his Bible. "Uh-huh. That way, when the bad guys lost, Israel knew it wasn't them. God did it. Because they asked Him."

I flipped the pillow on the bed. "I play trombone in the school band."

"Cool. Bring it next time. I'm gonna start trumpet

150

lessons. Mary Jane has a flute, Bonkers plays saxophone, an' Jig and Jag like to whack away on drums, and Lauren plays a clarinet."

I nodded. "Yeah, that would scare an army, all right. But what about now?"

"We could ask Ma if she'd let us load birthday candles in the empty chocolate milk pitchers, and smash the pitchers. Ya gotta let your light shine."

"Your mom's not going to let us break dishes." I flopped onto the bed. "We're doing this wrong."

Bash dropped onto his pillow. "Yeah. We have chocolate milk glass you can see through. You can't hide birthday candles inside."

"Not that. We're shooting darts and water because we're scared of a robber—"

"I'm not scared."

"Okay, in case we run into the robber. But we're not doing what the bug did."

"Sit on the pollywog tank to eat a frog?"

I threw my pillow at Bash. "No. We didn't pray."

"Praying mantises aren't really praying, you know. It just looks like it."

"I know. What I mean is the bug made me think. We're supposed to tell God everything, right? Like Gideon's people did."

Bash slid his Bible onto his chest. "I think I've got that marked in the Farmin' and Fishin' Book." He leafed pages, stopping at bookmarks, dried leaves, baseball cards, and scraps of paper. "Nope. Not that one. Not that one either. Here it is, right before the Lord's Prayer."

He propped the Bible on his chest with his torch hand and traced the words with his trumpet hand:

"'When you pray, don't babble like idol lovers—'"

I held up my hand. "I think the word is 'idolaters.'"

"Same thing. It's people who whine, and complain, and beg, but not to God."

I scratched my head. "I guess so."

Bash poked at his Bible and started reading again:

"'—don't babble like idol lovers, since they imagine they'll be heard for their many words. Don't be like them, because your Father knows the things you need before you ask Him.'"

Bash looked up. "That's Matthew, chapter six, verses seven and eight."

I pushed my glasses up the bridge of my nose. "Wasn't there a verse about asking, and looking, and finding?"

"Oh yeah, that one. It was one of our memory verses." Bash scrunched his eyes closed and chewed on his tongue for about five seconds. He stared at the ceiling, like he was reading the words in the paint:

"'Keep asking, and it will be given to you. Keep searching, and you will find. Keep knocking, and the door will be opened to you.' Matthew, chapter seven, verse seven."

I picked up the basketball. "Yeah, that's it."

Bash rolled over and flipped a page in his Bible.

"It also says in the Farmin' and Fishin' Book that when we don't get things, it's because we never asked, or we asked for stuff that's no good for us."

"Well, being protected from the robber is good for us. So let's ask."

"Good plan." Bash rolled over and looked up at the ceiling again. "Hi, God, it's me, Bash. Please keep us, and our chocolate, safe from the robber. Except the chocolate milk. He can have that."

I parked the basketball on my pillow, folded my hands, and bowed my head like the praying mantis. "Dear Jesus, make the robber get caught so he stops taking stuff from people. Don't let him hurt any of our friends. They're Your friends too."

Bash sat up. "Thanks, God. You're awesome."

I nodded. "Thank You, Jesus." I unfolded my hands. "He'll answer our prayers, won't He?"

Bash picked up the dart gun and water pellet gun, and tossed them into the closet. "He always does." Bash slammed the closet door. "The best part is He hardly ever answers exactly the way we think He should. Sometimes, He tells us to grab a birthday candle in our left hand, a kazoo in our right, smash chocolate milk pitchers, and stand in front of billions of bad guys. It's way cooler."

God wouldn't do that to us. Would He?

Chapter 17

Any Quilt in a Storm

Prickles scampered in tiny icicles across the back of my neck. A gush of cold wind blew goose bumps down my arms. I bit my lower lip, closed one eye, and peeked at the sky. Big, black clouds barged across it like waves crashing onto a sandy beach. I shivered. It looked nasty.

I shook Bash's shoulder. "Um, shouldn't we, uh, you know, go inside?"

My lunatic cousin sat in the gravel driveway, drawing another tic-tac-toe board in the dirt. Uncle Jake pawed at a bug beside him. Bash scratched Uncle Jake's ears. "Nah.

Feels like rain. Rain means mud ball fights." Bash tapped the tic-tac-toe scratchings. "Your turn to go first."

Another layer of black clouds crowded the late Friday morning sky. The air rumbled. I drew an *O* in the upper right square. "Your driveway mud's full of pebbles. You're not thinking of beaning me with stones, are you?"

Bash squinted at me. "You're supposed to duck. Don't you know anything about mud ball fights?" He scraped an *X* in the upper left square.

Uncle Jake curled around my legs and slurped my cheek. I picked up a stick, etched another *O* right below my first one, and threw the stick for Uncle Jake to chase. "I know our moms always get upset when we wear more mud than clothes."

"Which is why you have mud ball fights in the rain." Bash blocked me with an *X* in the bottom right corner. "The rain washes the mud away. It's simple."

"We're supposed to be washing Morton."

"You can't wash a goat in the rain. He'd get wet."

"He's supposed to get wet. We're washing him."

Another boom echoed. It sounded closer. Uncle Jake dropped the stick at my feet and scampered toward the house. I hurried an *O* in the bottom left corner of the tic-tac-toe board. "Hey, look, here comes your dad on the John Deere. He's not going to stay outside. Let's go in."

Bash shook his head. He scrawled an *X* in the middle square to both block me and to win driveway tic-tac-toe for the forty-seventh time in a row since I showed up on Monday. "You make it too easy, Beamer. That's fifty-four games in a row for me. Thunder got ya nervous?"

Yes. "No." I gulped and glanced at the darkening clouds. "Thunder's just noise. It's the lightning that worries me. And it's only forty-seven in a row."

"One of us doesn't count very well." Bash grinned and wiped out the tic-tac-toe board. He drew fresh hash marks in the dirt. "Goin' for fifty-five. Pops'll probably work in the tractor barn a while. Somethin' always needs fixin' out there."

Uncle Rollie nodded as he barreled past us on his big green tractor. "Rain," he shouted above the roar.

"Yeah," Bash yelled back with a thumbs-up and a goofy grin. He drew an *X* in the center square.

"See," I said. "Your dad told us to go inside. And this is forty-eight. I mean, forty-seven for you and one for me. I'm the guy who can count, remember?"

"Not hardly. And Pops said it's gonna rain. Rain's good. It's your turn."

A big, fat raindrop cracked like an egg on top of my head. Another juicy drop washed out Bash's *X*.

Lightning exploded like the flash of a zillion cell phone cameras. I jumped to my feet.

Ka-BOOM. When the thunder blammed liked a thousand tractors crashing, I took it as the starting gun and ran.

"Forfeit!" Bash yelled. "That's fifty-five to zero." But I heard him forfeiting right behind me, crashing through the sudden wall of rain.

I yanked open the screen door of the back porch mudroom, and we dove inside just as another crackle of lightning fired another shot. I rammed into a soaking wet Uncle Rollie and bounced to the floor, tripping Bash, who crashed on top of me in time with the boom of thunder.

Uncle Rollie grinned down at us. "What took you boys so long?" He took off his soppy baseball cap and flicked rainwater at us. "Nothing like a spring thunderstorm, is there?"

"I wouldn't say nothin'," Bash said. "We must get like twenty or thirty good ones every spring."

"Not hardly that many, Champ. We get some doozies, but I don't think you count very well."

"See." I pushed Bash's knee away from my mouth. "Now get off me."

"Oops, sorry, Beams." Bash planted his other knee into my shoulder and pushed himself up, only clopping me once with his foot.

"Thanks a lot," I muttered.

Uncle Rollie hung his ball cap on a hook and plopped into a beat-up porch chair to unlace his work boots. "Guess you know where I'll be."

"Sure, Pops. I'll get your quilt."

I stumbled to my feet and followed Bash into the house. "Your dad hides under the bed during storms?"

"Nah. Why'd you say that?"

"You said you were getting his quilt. I figured he must be going to bed. But in a storm like this, it's smarter to crawl under the bed."

Bash snatched an old, ratty blanket with a couple of holes in it off the back of Uncle Rollie's easy chair. I followed Bash out the front door and onto the big porch. Bash tossed the lumpy blanket onto the hanging porch swing. Even at this far end of the porch, wind gusts misted us with dribbles from the crashing rain.

I flinched when another jagged blade of lightning ripped a hole through the sky. "Why are we out here?"

"Because it's raining," Bash said.

The front door opened and Uncle Rollie, in slippers, picked up the blanket and flipped it over his shoulders. He wrapped it around him like a cocoon and thumped onto the porch swing. "Ahhh. Now that feels good."

He closed his eyes and grinned as spits of rain misted his face. Extra folds of the blanket flapped beside him. The swing creaked as he rocked: *Squeeee, squaawwwww, squeeee, squaawwwww.*

I nudged Bash and whispered, "What's he doing?"

Bash snapped open a folding chair and settled into it. He whispered: "Swinging. What are you doing?"

A long, jagged streak of lightning crackled a rip through the purple sky. A rumble bounced across the clouds. Rain poured. I scratched my head, which sent a small shower of trapped rain down my nose. "I don't know what anybody's doing."

The screen door *sproinged* open. Aunt Tillie, also in slippers, stepped out, holding the door back with her hip while she carried a tray. She let Darla and Uncle Jake dash around her before she let the screen door wham shut. "Have some coffee, Roland?"

Uncle Rollie slid a purple mug off the tray. "Thanks, Mattie."

Another flash. Another *kaboom.* This time, it rattled my chest.

Aunt Tillie set the tray on a plastic end table beside the porch swing. She picked up two large glasses of chocolate milk. "Here you go, boys. Just the thing for rain watching."

Bash shook his head. "No thanks, Ma. I'm good."

Uncle Rollie raised his eyebrows. "I believe, Bash, you meant to say, 'Thank you, Mom, and I'll have some more when I finish this glass.'"

Bash gulped. "Oh, yeah. Chocolate milk. My favorite. Thanks, Ma."

Uncle Jake sauntered onto a throw rug in front of Bash's chair, circled three times, and plopped down. He rested his red head on his paws and watched the rain.

I opened another folding chair and scooted in beside Bash. My nose crinkled when I lifted a glass of chocolate milk from the tray. Now that we could have all the chocolate milk we wanted, I didn't want very much. I set the distasteful cup beside me on the porch. Maybe I could figure out how to spill it into the bushes when nobody was looking.

Uncle Rollie tipped his mug to his lips. "Oh, you boys best be careful. We wouldn't want those cups accidentally getting knocked over. Mattie's forsythia bushes prefer rainwater to chocolate milk."

I think I did, too, but I didn't mention it.

Aunt Tillie set her own mug of coffee on another table. Uncle Rollie held open the blanket. She snuggled in beside him, and Darla crawled onto his lap. Uncle Rollie again closed the cocoon and rocked. *Squeeee, squaawwwww, squeeee, squaawwwww.* Lightning flashed, thunder boomed, rain fell. *Squeeee, squaawwwww, squeeee, squaawwwww.*

I leaned toward Bash and whispered. "Seriously, what are we doing?"

Bash plugged his nose and sipped chocolate milk. "What's it look like? We're watching the rain."

Flash. *Kerrrack.* A river of water flowed down the drive. "Why?"

Bash shrugged. "I dunno. Pops loves to watch thunderstorms."

Lightning. "Um, wouldn't it be better to watch it in the car? Dale Huston from school told me that rubber tires eat lightning."

A corner of Uncle Rollie's mustache rose. "Well, Raymond, you're certainly welcome to wait out the storm riding a bicycle. Two tires ought to be enough to protect one boy."

Sheets of rain half hid the Gobnotters' farm down the road. The pelting on the aluminum roof of the porch sounded like a hundred Bashes spilling frozen peas on a drum. It looked wet. I reached for my chocolate milk. "Um, no thanks."

Uncle Rollie, Aunt Tillie, and Darla rocked. *Squeeee, squaawwwww, squeeee, squaawwwww.* Uncle Rollie ruffled Darla's hair. "'Tain't the tires, anyway. It's the metal framing of the car. It conducts the juice around the outside of the passenger compartment, away from you, and pulls it down to the road. Small chance your car will ever be hit."

Bash chewed his tongue for a moment. "So, Pops, what happens if lightning makes a direct hit on a tire?"

"The tire blows up, I reckon."

Bash chomped his tongue harder. "So if I had all the kids bring over their toasters, an' we wired a thousand toasters to the truck tire, an' they all popped at once—"

Aunt Tillie's eyelid wound up for takeoff. "Sebastian Nicholas Hinglehobb, you will *not* hook up perfectly good toasters to a perfectly good tire . . ." Her eyelid began jumping. "Roland, talk to your son."

Uncle Rollie chuckled and squeezed Aunt Tillie's shoulder. He winked at Bash. "First of all, Champ, leave my truck tires out of your schemes. If you want to blow up tires, buy your own. Which you can't, because for the next year, you're paying for a whole tank of ruined milk."

Aunt Tillie's eye tic picked up the pace. "Roland!"

"And secondly, I believe we discussed this the last time. No more toaster experiments. They're pert near as dangerous as kissing an angry bull on the nose. You blew every breaker in the house that time."

Bash slumped in his chair. "Oh, yeah. I forgot."

Lightning. Thunder.

Aunt Tillie cupped a hand over her eye. "Four years hasn't been long enough for me to forget."

"Plus, the toast never tasted the same," Uncle Rollie said.

I leaned toward Bash and whispered. "What did you do?"

He shrugged. "I don't wanna talk about it. 'Sides, I was only seven. An' my eyebrows grew back."

"Your eyebrows—" I jumped as another bolt of lightning caught me by surprise. I felt the metal frame of the folding chair. I yelled above the thudding of the thunder. "Why are we watching a thunderstorm?"

Uncle Rollie rocked. *Squeeee, squaawwwww, squeeee, squaawwwww.* "It's relaxing."

"It is?" I'd been clenching every muscle I knew how to clench since the first rumble. There's nothing relaxing about thunder and lightning.

Another jerky line of lightning tore the sky and appeared to stab the woods. I flinched, expecting the trees to explode. *Ka-Boom*. Not the trees. Just thunder. Like a gunshot. My lip quivered. "Did they catch the robber?"

Chapter 18

Mud Fight!

"I reported those footprints you found. Deputies swept the woods. They found where he was. Now it's where he isn't." Uncle Rollie sipped his coffee. "Until we know if he's gone for good, Frank and Joe, stay out of the woods."

Bash looked puzzled. "Who?"

I swirled my chocolate milk. "The Hardy Boys."

Bash scratched his ear. "Who?"

"Frank and Joe Hardy. Teenage detectives. They have lots of books." Bash shook his head at each sentence. I sighed. "Forget it. What your dad means is no mystery solving."

"Then how are we supposed to investigate?"

"We're not."

Uncle Jake yawned, shook his doggy head, settled it back onto his paws, and sighed himself to sleep. Uncle Rollie slid a burly arm around Aunt Tillie's shoulder, and hugged her into him. Their heads made a tent over Darla's hair. "I don't know if he's skedaddled. What I do know is when it rains like this, I can't work in the fields. And if I'm caught up enough on my barn work, I get to sit on the porch and relax for a few minutes."

"You could play video games. Or watch TV. That's relaxing. Inside. Away from the lightning."

"I reckon we're watching quite a show right here." Uncle Rollie tugged at his mustache. "Have you ever considered the sheer power of water?"

I was too busy considering the sheer power of lightning.

Uncle Rollie stretched his legs. "Without the rain, my hay, soybeans, oats, and corn won't grow. Water is life. But too much rain washes seeds out of the fields, or rots the plants. Water can destroy. Strong stuff, rain is."

Bash gagged down another gulp of chocolate milk. He wiped his arm across his mouth. "Nothin' better than chocolate milk, I always say. Right, Pops?"

Uncle Rollie winked at me. "Help yourself. We seem to have plenty, for some odd reason."

The rumbles lessened, and the rain settled into a gentler *rat-a-tat-tat-tat* on the roof. Actually, the cool mist tickling my face from gust to gust wasn't all that bad. "So is rain good or bad?"

Uncle Rollie rocked. *Squeeee, squaawwwww, squeeee,*

squaawwwww. "Way I figure it, God made it, so it's good. But that first rainfall wiped out everything on earth except Noah, his family, and the animals God sent to the massive boat Noah built. God used the water from above and gushing up from below to cleanse the land. But I don't 'spect the people left behind cared for it very much."

I glugged chocolate milk and sank a bit into my chair. "But you like rain?"

"Can't farm without it."

"Don't forget the vegetable garden. No rain, no green beans," Aunt Tillie said.

I scowled.

"Some people happen to like green beans," she said. "And my flowers look so vibrant after a good soaking."

Uncle Rollie nodded. "But given enough time, rushing water will carve right through rocks. Ever wonder why the stones at the bottom of the creek are so smooth? Water wears away the rough edges."

I swished chocolate milk around in my cheeks. Swallowed. Wiped my mouth. And wondered about water. "So, is that what baptism is? Washing away the rough edges?"

Squeeee, squaawwwww, squeeee, squaawwwww.

"Not exactly," Aunt Tillie said.

Uncle Rollie set his coffee mug on a plastic side table, and pulled a battered New Testament from his front pocket. "Let's see, I believe it's when Peter is talking about Noah and the ark . . ." He flipped pages. "Here we go, 1 Peter 3:20–21: '. . . God patiently waited in the days of Noah while an ark was being prepared. In it a few—that is, eight people—were saved through water. Baptism, which corresponds to this, now saves you (not the removal of the filth of the flesh, but the pledge of a good conscience toward God) through the resurrection of Jesus Christ.'"

I scratched my head. "Um, okay."

Uncle Rollie chuckled. "It's not the water, it's Jesus. He cleans us. Baptism is how we identify with Him."

Bash emptied his chocolate milk in one final gasp, clutched his throat, and set down the empty cup. "Plus rain makes great mud. The best mud ball fights come from rain."

The lightning and thunder had quit. The rain settled into a soft, spring shower. I watched water cascade from the beginnings of spring leaves on the maple and birch trees like at one of those fancy fountains in the mall. Glistening grass danced under the drops. Glimmers of sunlight flickered through the clouds. The washing of rain on the roof sounded so . . . so . . . I settled back, folded my arms over my stomach, closed my eyes, and tried to figure out what baptism meant.

I didn't get it. So water cleans, but it doesn't clean us. I sighed and listened to the rain in the cool breezes. I wished for a blanket. God saved Noah with lots of water, but it was God, not the water. It was just so—

Splat!

My eyes shot open, but I couldn't see. A glob of mud dripped down my forehead. I smeared it away just in time for another mud ball to plunk me in the chest. *Whap!*

Bash stood in the rain at the edge of the porch, mud washing through his fingers. "Told ya. Rain makes the best mud balls." Uncle Jake circled around Bash's legs, his red doggy hair dripping with rain, his tongue and tail wagging.

I burst off the porch. Bash took off on a dead run. I

zipped through the nearest mud puddle, grabbed a slop of slime, and charged.

"Stop before you poke an eye out," Aunt Tillie hollered.

I hesitated. Uncle Rollie chuckled. "Let 'em go, Mattie. They're boys. Besides, rain may not clean the insides, but water does a great job of washing mud away."

So I flung gunk at Bash. He popped from behind a tree and slapped a handful of mud on my back. "Gotcha again!"

I twisted and tackled him. We rolled through rain, wet grass, and mud puddles, laughing and yelling and burbling. Uncle Jake barked, jumped, and splashed right along beside us, hitting the puddles we missed. There's nothing like a good mud bath—especially when you get to give one to your cousin.

"Tic-tac-toe this, buddy!" I dived on Mudman Bash.

Splaaaaat!

"Not today, Drippy Drawers." Bash grabbed my ankles and flipped me onto my back.

Sploooosh!

A shout interrupted the next good splashdown. "Boys!" Aunt Tillie stood at the edge of the porch. "It stopped raining."

Water still cascaded from my fingers. All from the mud puddle. I stared at the sky. When had the sun come out?

Bash sat up in a mud puddle. Brown water dripped from matted hair that used to be the color of straw. "But there're still lots of mud puddles, Ma. A whole driveway full of 'em."

"Go hose yourselves off. And then you have a goat to wash." Aunt Tillie pointed up. "I believe it looks something like that rainbow."

An arch of colors glittered in the late morning sky.

"God's promise," Uncle Rollie said. "He told Noah in Genesis that the rainbow would be a sign of His promise to never destroy the whole earth with a flood again."

I sat in the water and stared. When God signs a promise, He sure knows how to make His signature stand out.

Uncle Rollie helped Aunt Tillie gather mugs and cups. "Better hop to it, boys. That old goat isn't going to wash himself."

I shuddered. "Maybe the rain already did it and we don't have to go."

Bash squeezed water out of his shirt. "Nope. Morton hates rain. He always hides in his tree hutch."

I flicked mud globs from my jeans. "What about Mary Jane?"

"Nope. She woulda stayed in the store."

"Not that. What's she going to do to us?"

Bash gave the puddle one last stomp. "Nothing, if all the paint washes off."

"And if it doesn't?"

"We better find the robber."

"Why?"

"To ask if he has extra room in his hideout. We'll need it."

Chapter 19

Stick 'Em Up!

Never had I been assigned a mission so dangerous, so death-defying, so absolutely insane.

Aunt Tillie ordered us to go to the store. Morrises' store. By ourselves. Where Mary Jane ruled from a stool behind the iron cash register. To wash a goat. Mary Jane's goat. That we painted.

If I met the robber himself, it couldn't be any worse.

I barely heard my thoughts over the *crunkety-crunk-crunk* of the red wagon on the damp roadside gravel. "How come your mom makes us pull this wagon like we're little kids?"

Bash's cheek bobbled like a cat in a paper bag. This could be the time he chewed his tongue right off. "She needs some groceries while we're there. She doesn't want to hear you whine about how heavy the stuff was to carry the half mile home."

"You're the whiner." I picked a couple empty bottles and a shoe out of the ditch, shook off the rainwater, and dropped them in the wagon beside the soap, bucket, rags, and scrub brushes. I'd throw the trash away at the store. "We could have harnessed Gully to the wagon again. The pork could pull."

Bash scooped up a single, soggy glove and tossed it in the wagon. "Not a good idea to tie Gulliver J. McFrederick the Third to a wagon full of food. Last time, he dumped the wagon, broke a jar of pickles, and ate half a bag of muffins before I could stop him."

The wagon *crunkety-crunk-crunked*. The bottles *clackety-clack-clacked*. My heart *thumpety-thump-thumped*.

"Bash."

"Yeah, Beamer."

"Do you suppose Mary Jane still wants to clobber us?"

"She always wants to clobber me."

Crunkety-crunk-crunk. Clackety-clack-clack. Thumpety-thump-thump.

"It was my idea to spray-paint her goat. Well, not the goat exactly, but my idea."

"Yeah, I said get the goat." Bash chewed his tongue a bit longer. "It was a good gag to go out on if, well, you know."

"If what?"

"If Mary Jane doesn't grow a sense of humor in the next five minutes."

Crunkety-crunk-crunk. Clackety-clack-clack. Thumpety-thump-thump.

I glanced ahead at Morrises' Corner Store and Seed Emporium. "She's got a good sense of a right hook. Or is that a left jab?"

Bash rubbed his shoulder and shuddered. "Both."

"Maybe she won't be working today."

Bash chewed. "She always minds the cash register on Friday afternoons. It's when her folks take stuff to the food bank an' make deliveries."

"Oh."

Crunkety-crunk-crunk. Clackety-clack-clack. Thumpety-thump-thump.

"Her folks shouldn't leave her alone. What if the robber runs into the store and yells, 'Stick 'em up?'"

"Nobody yells stick 'em up. C'mon, Beamer, grow up."

I grabbed a wad of newspapers and a crumpled candy wrapper from the ditch and added them to the trash in the wagon. "How do you know what robbers yell? Have you ever been stuck up?"

"I'm not stuck up. It's just crazy, that's all."

"Well, her folks shouldn't leave her unguarded. She could hurt somebody. Like us."

Bash dug a chipped marble out of the gravel, started to plink it toward the wagon, stopped, and shoved the broken marble in his pocket instead. "She's not alone. The Gobnotter farm is just across the road. Scream loud enough, and Jig, Jag or their pops will come rescue you."

"I don't need to be rescued from Mary Jane. You do."

"Whose paint was it?"

My stomach lurched.

Crunkety-crunk-crunk. Clackety-clack-clack. Thumpety-thump-thump.

We shuffled into the parking lot and left the wagon by the front steps. I stared at the wood-frame screen door. "You go in. I'll take care of the trash." I grabbed bottles and newspaper from the wagon and headed toward the recycling bin next to the flower pots.

"I better help." Bash bundled up the candy wrapper, glove, and tattered shoe, and stuffed them into the trash. In seconds, we had the wagon cleaned out except for the Morton-cleaning supplies.

I bumped Bash toward the store door. "Go on, open it."

Bash zipped behind me. "Goat painting was your idea. You open the door."

"My idea was to paint you. You said paint the goat." I dragged him back in front. "You go first."

"It was your paint."

"It's your mom's shopping list."

Bash circled behind me and pushed me in the back. "With that burglar running around, somebody ought to stay outside and guard the wagon. I better do it since I'm bravest."

I kicked a block step. "If you're bravest, you go in. She's just a girl."

Bash looked up at the door. "Nope. That's not a girl. It's Mary Jane."

Wham! The screen door crashed open. We jumped. Mary Jane stood there, holding the door back, the business end of her pointy-toed cowboy boots pointing their pointy toes right at us.

Bash doffed his baseball cap. "Hi, Mary Jane. Is that a new dress?"

"It's not new, and it's not a dress, Sebastian Nicholas Hinglehobb." Her head shifted. Blue eyes lasered into me. I gulped. She glared. "Well, Raymond William Boxby, do you care to take a shot at what I'm wearing?"

I gulped again. "A skirt? A jumper? Culottes?" I threw up my hands. "Look, we're just here for stuff for Aunt Tillie. We don't even have to go in. You take the list and the money. Just put the stuff in the wagon. We'll wait across the road at Jig and Jag's farm. Okay?"

Her eyebrows narrowed. A brown curl slid over her shoulder and swung free like a dangling noose. "You mean you'll go out back and wash the paint off Morton, right?"

Bash nodded. "Sure, MJ. Look, we got soap and brushes in the wagon. We'll just turn on the hose and be on our way. Bye."

"Hold it." She stepped back. "Customers may enter. As long as said customers hold no paint cans or coloring sets."

"We don't have any of those, Mary Jane. At least, I don't. Maybe you better check Beamer." Bash shot past her and into the store.

I stood at the bottom of the steps. Mary Jane stood inside the door at the top. Neither of us moved. I gulped again. My throat was beginning to hurt from gulping. "Look, Mary Jane, it was an April Fool's joke. I only used hair coloring that washes right out. It says so on the can. Washes right out in the shower."

"Have you ever tried to get a goat to stand still in a shower?"

"Um, no."

"You're going to learn." She disappeared into the depths of the store, letting the screen door slam behind her. I figured I'd just stay outside and guard the wagon in case the burglar showed up. But the door popped open again. Bash waved me in. "Beams, c'mon. Mary Jane went behind the counter. She's not going to flatten you. You're clear—as long as the paint comes off Morty-Orty-Applesauce-Sorty. Help me get Ma's stuff."

I sucked in a double lungful of air, held it, then let it hiss out. I figured her folks wouldn't let Mary Jane take free hits on customers. I climbed the two steps and pushed open the door.

The bare, buckled wooden floor creaked as I tip-toed to join Bash. Like always, the store smelled like a mixture of spilt flour, dusty burlap feed sacks, and molasses. The shelves of the little store held an odd assortment of groceries and country things—loaves of bread, snack cakes, cereals, soup, root beer mix, baseball cards, balsa wood airplanes, paraffin, canning jars and lids, flypaper, udder cream, and even a broken horse halter hanging from a nail. The Morrises kept the sacks of seeds for gardens and fields in a small, tilted barn out back.

I stepped behind Bash, so as to keep him between me and Mary Jane, and peeked over his shoulder at the list. "So what are we picking up?"

"Let's see, Ma needs a jar of hot pepper mustard, a bucket of laundry soap, a five-pound bag of steel-cut oats, some apple-cinnamon pancake mix—"

"*Blech.* She really doesn't like us, does she?"

"Apple-cinnamon pancakes aren't so bad."

"They are with chocolate milk. And in case you've forgotten, chocolate is *all* we get to drink anymore."

Bash groaned. "Yeah, I had to get up three times in the middle of the night, once for each glass of chocolate milk I had to drink before bed. You?"

I grimaced. "Five times. I can't believe your mom even made the macaroni and cheese for lunch today with chocolate milk. Cheddar and chocolate—total gross-out."

Bash slumped against a shelf of honey butter and clutched his stomach. "Ugh. Don't remind me."

Broooinnng. The spring played its odd tune as someone opened the screen door. A guy in a ratty jacket stood in the doorway and blinked his eyes.

"May I help you, sir?" Mary Jane cooed.

"In a minute." The guy stood on tiptoe to see across the store. He walked past me to turn down the bread aisle. *Woo-wee.* He smelled like someone had dressed a pig and a chicken in old sweat socks and grungy basketball shorts and let them ripen inside in a middle school gym locker for six months.

He wandered to the door at the back that opened into the other half of the building, the part where the Morrises lived. I peeked around the aisle to see where he went.

"Heads up, Beamer."

"Wha . . . ?" I turned just in time to see a jar sailing toward me. "Yipe." I ducked.

A jam jar sailed over my head. *Crassshhhsplottt.* The jar smashed on the bumpy hardwood floor. Orange marmalade oozed like spreading fire.

Mary Jane shrieked. "You clean up that mess right now, Sebastian Nicholas Hinglehobb!"

"It's not my fault. Beamer ducked."

"You threw marmalade at me."

"I was throwing it *to* you. It's on Ma's list. You were supposed to catch it."

Mary Jane powered around the counter and burrowed her nose right into Bash's. "And you are going to pay for that."

Bash gulped. "Can't. I lost my allowance 'cause of the chocolate milk. How 'bout some more chocolate milk?"

"How about if I—"

"Knock it off." The shabby man stood with hands over his ears.

Mary Jane backed up a step. Her cheeks flushed. "I'm sorry, sir. May I help you with something while these boys clean up the orange marmalade?"

The man shuffled forward. I sniffed. Not dirty sweat socks so much as wet leaves, dirt, and moss. I hoped he'd ask for deodorant soap.

He jerked a thumb toward the back of the store. "Your folks at home?"

"Mom was called away on an emergency at Aunt Sarah's. Dad needed to deliver bread to Mrs. Kaupila, who broke her leg and can't get out. He'll be back in fifteen minutes. My big brother just left for baseball practice so he wouldn't be late."

The man leaned for a better look past the bread shelves. "Any adults left who I can talk to?"

Mary Jane glared at us. "The only two human beings under this roof are you and me. Those two little kids don't count."

The guy wandered up to the counter. My eyes watered as he walked by. Mary Jane hurried around to her stool behind the cash register. Her nose twitched. Bash coughed. The guy smelled like he'd been living in the woods for four weeks.

Uh-oh.

I looked at his feet. Big. Like the footprints . . . in the woods.

Oh no. I hated finding clues.

I waved for Mary Jane's attention and pointed at the guy's feet. She ignored me. "What may I do for you, sir?"

He reached into his coat pocket. "Stick 'em up."

Bash rolled his eyes. "Seriously? Stick 'em up? Do robbers still say that?"

The smelly man shrugged and drew his hand out of his pocket.

He held a gun.

Chapter 20

Gideon's Kazoo Meets the Goat of Many Colors

The orange tip of the stubby black muzzle swung at us. "Tweedledum. Tweedledee. Get over here where I can see you." We parked ourselves next to the marmalade lava flow.

The gun guy turned to Mary Jane. "Look, I'm going to need you to empty that cash register."

Mary Jane quivered. "You're . . . you're robbing me?"

"Yeah, I'm sorry about that. Really, I am. But I need just a little more cash. I hate sleeping in the woods. I want a motel. And Twinkies. Got any with chocolate filling?"

Mary Jane wrinkled her nose and coughed. "A shower would be nice."

"No dramatics, kid. Just empty that cash register. How old is that thing, anyway?"

Mary Jane's hand trembled as she punched a key on the big, black iron cash register. The cash drawer shot out with a *cha-ching*. "Daddy . . . Daddy found it at a flea market. He says it's from 1910. He—Please don't do this, sir."

Tink, tink, tunk, tink. The guy tapped the stubby end of the gun against the counter. "Empty the dollars right here. You can keep the change."

My knees knocked. I didn't know knees actually knocked. I thought it was a made-up thing comic book guys drew, because there's always a picture of the guy with knees knocking when the scary thing shows up, and I thought it was silly, and I'd always laugh, but now the scary thing was in front of me, my knees clattered, and . . .

I jumped when Bash cleared his throat. His knees didn't knock, but he'd lost his tan. "Mister, I gotta know. Am I . . . Am I Tweedledum or Tweedledee?"

I stared at Bash. So did the gunman and Mary Jane. Bash's white face turned red. He shuffled. "I want to be Tweedledee. Beamer can be Tweedledum."

The gun guy rolled his eyes. Mary Jane spilled dollars onto the counter.

Tweedledum—or possibly Tweedledee, the gun guy never said which of us was which—began to pray silently. *God, help. Gun, gun, gun. Help, oh no, help, help. God, help us. Please, please, please. Oh no, oh no, oh no.* Hey, I was stressed. But I knew it was okay. When Jesus is your best friend, when you talk with Him all day long inside your heart, you don't lose a lot of time introducing yourself when you need to talk to Him in a hurry.

I sure hoped Bash remembered to pray. He's the one who taught me. I tried to slide to my left to nudge Bash, but my foot stuck. I looked down. My sneaker squished the gooey middle of fiery orange marmalade splattered from a broken jar. Sort of like birthday candles flaming from a broken chocolate milk pitcher. I choked back a giggle.

Bash furrowed his brow as if to ask, "What?"

"Kazoo," I whispered.

The robber stirred the wad of dollar bills with the orange tip of his gun. "That's not very much, kid."

Mary Jane rattled the cash drawer. "But I . . . See . . . That's all that's in the drawer."

I raised my hand. "Mister. I know where there's more."

The robber, Bash, and Mary Jane all stared at me. I cleared my throat. "I know where she hides the rest of it."

Mary Jane gasped. The robber scratched his head with the gun. "In a safe, no doubt."

"No. In a tree. Well, under a tree stump."

It was Mary Jane's turn to go white. "Raymond William Boxby, don't you dare . . ."

The robber stuffed the bills on the counter into his jacket pockets. "You don't say. Where is this tree?"

"Out back. In the pasture. I'll show you."

Mary Jane lunged over the counter at me. "Don't!"

But I already moved toward the door, leaving a sticky trail of fiery orange marmalade and glass shards behind. You could practically see the smoke billowing out Mary Jane's ears right through her curls.

The gun guy arched an eyebrow. "You're going to blow a gasket, kid." He shrugged and waved his gun. "Okay, let's go. All of you. But nobody better make a break for it."

I led the eager robber, a curious Bash, and a furious Mary Jane out the screen door, around the side of the store, and to the back. I unlatched the pasture gate. "This way. See the rock at the base of the stump over there. It's covering a hole."

Mary Jane bumped me. "I'll get you for this, Raymond William Boxby."

But the beginnings of a smile trembled across Bash's face. "Gideon's kazoo."

The robber narrowed his eyes. "What?"

Bash bobbed his head. "Yep, that's the stump, Mister. Mary Jane showed us herself. She started hiding it there because a robber was running around these parts. I guess that would be you, huh? Want me to hold your gun?"

"Nice try, kid." The robber stuffed the gun in his jacket pocket. "You three stand over there where I can see you. Move."

We went. Mary Jane stomped on Bash's foot as she marched past him to stand at the end of the line.

The robber poked at the rock with his foot.

Bash nodded. "That's it."

"Yeah," I said. "You gotta bend way over to dig into the hole, but there's a big ol' bag of money down there, I bet."

Mary Jane side-kicked Bash. She couldn't reach me. "Shut up, you two. Whose side are you on?"

The robber pushed the stone away with his foot. He

studied the three of us to make sure we were far enough away. First he peered down his nose at the hole. And squinted. He leaned down a little. Dropped to his knees. "Yuck. The ground's still wet." He sprang into a crouch. Then bent way over to poke a hand inside.

It looked sorta like a football lineman's stance.

"Time to play the trumpet," I whispered.

"Naah-aaah-aaah," Bash coughed softly in his best goat voice.

Two eyes peered from the hutch tucked into a tree. Then a goat's head. Then the full, painted goat.

Mary Jane's eyebrows popped up. She'd figured it out. And she grinned.

Morton trotted down limbs and tree house ramp.

"Got it." The robber, his back to us, pulled a bank bag out of the stump.

Morton dropped to the ground. His nostrils quivered. His head lowered.

"Anything else in here?" The crouching robber stretched. His backside wriggled. Morton took it for an invitation.

I whispered, "Hike."

In a blur of circus colors, the goat of many colors charged. Streaks of greens, blues, reds, yellows, purples, and oranges flashed across the pasture. *Naaaaaah-aaaah-aaaaah!* It was head-butting time. Except that if Morton had been aiming for the robber's head, the robber would have seen Morty charging. Morton wasn't and the robber didn't.

Whump!

Touchdown, Morton.

Krunk!

The gun guy smacked the tree stump. He toddled there, head down against the stump, backside waving high.

Morton backed up and *whumped* him again. *Krunk!* This time, the leaning guy shuddered, paused, then tipped like a chopped tree. *Whoomf!* He tumbled onto his side, out cold.

Mary Jane leaped to Morton's side and sniffled into his neck. "Good boy, Morton. Oh, my Morty-Morton-Orton. Good boy."

Morton chewed the flappy elbow of the robber's jacket. *"Maaa-haa-haa-haa-haaa."*

Bash whooped and slapped me with a high-five.

I hugged Morton. "Just like Gideon's guys. Morton used his ram's horn."

"He's not a ram," Mary Jane said. "Male sheep are rams. Morton's a goat. He's a buck."

"Whatever. It worked. Thank You, God." I looked around the pasture. "Rope. We need to tie him up."

"Got it." Bash sprinted to the garden hose, whipped out his pocketknife and sliced off half the hose.

"Not the garden hose!" Mary Jane wailed.

I gaped at Bash. "You had your knife this whole time? Why didn't you defend us?"

"Pops says it's a farmin' tool, never, ever to be used as a weapon. 'Sides, if he'd shot my pocketknife, it might rust."

"Huh?"

"Water rusts pocketknives."

"What water?"

"The squirt gun."

"What squirt gun?"

"The robber's. Didn't you see it? He kept waving it around like he meant to soak somebody."

Mary Jane snatched the sliced hose from Bash's hand. "Give me that. If you two are going to stand there and argue, I better tie up this gentleman before he wakes up." She pulled his arms and legs behind him and began trussing up the gun guy like a rodeo calf. "I always wanted to try this."

I snatched a stick and tapped the gun that had fallen on the ground. *Ping, ping.* Plastic! I picked the gun and shook it. It sloshed. I tilted it just enough to see the end of the orange-tipped barrel. A squirt gun hole. I pulled the trigger. A stream of water splashed a clump of daisies.

I threw the gun down and whirled on Bash. "How'd you know?"

"I have one just like it, remember? We used it to mix colors when we painted Morty-Kanorty-Supergoat-Dorty. Plus, real guns don't drip."

"If you knew it was a squirt gun, why didn't you rush him?"

The Basher admired Mary Jane's calf-tying skills. "Well, he was a robber, you know. And he wanted Mary Jane's money, not mine."

Mary Jane cinched another knot in the garden hose and glared up at Bash. "You're a jerk, Sebastian Nicholas Hinglehobb. Go get help."

"I'll get Mr. Gobnotter 'cross the road." Bash sprinted through the open gate.

"Or you could call the sheriff," Mary Jane bellowed after him.

The squirt gun guy groaned. "Wha happened? Ooh, my head. My rear. What hit me?"

Mary Jane scratched behind Morton's ears as he munched on a piece of pocket he'd torn off the guy's coat. "A spray-painted goat. I must say, sir, he has very good aim."

The guy tried to move. His eyes bugged. "I'm paralyzed."

Mary Jane shook her head. "You're tied with garden hose. You might as well relax, sir."

The guy dropped his head on the ground. It must have reminded him that he had a goat-butting headache because he yelped. "Somebody call the sheriff. I'm ready to go in. Jail can't be worse than this."

"He's on his way, sir. Unless Sebastian Nicholas Hinglehobb got distracted again, in which case, I'll bring you a pillow."

Kerrrr-unnnk. Crunnncchhh. Kerrr-aaack.

The robber's eyes popped open. "What's that?"

I pointed at the rainbow goat. "Morton just ate your gun. That's destroying evidence. Now he's going to be arrested too. You guys can share a cell."

This time the robber didn't even wince when he dropped his head to the ground. He just cried.

Chapter 21

Pondwater Bathtub
for a Goat

Icy water nipped my toes. I back-pedaled so fast that I stumbled and nearly sat down hard on the pond bank. "It's too cold."

Mary Jane stood in the grass above the pond, her arms folded, one pointy-toed cowboy boot tapping. On her left, Jag glowered like nobody'd ever painted a goat before. On the other side of Mary Jane, Lauren bit a curving lip as if she remembered a really great joke but was trying to keep from laughing out loud in class.

I looked from the girls on shore to the water at my bare toes. I knew I wasn't going ashore. "Okay, but this is a lousy way to treat a bunch of heroes."

Deputies had rescued the robber about three hours earlier. They hadn't stayed around to rescue us. And since Bash had cut up the watering hose, Mary Jane marched us, goat, and scrub brushes to Bash's pond. The rest of the kids showed up after the sheriff's cars came. When the deputies left, the kids tagged along behind us, making it a circus farm parade, complete with clown goat.

Mary Jane uncrossed her arms and dug balled-up fists into her hips. "It's one of the warmest Aprils we've ever had. The water's fine. You're fine. Morton, however, is not fine. Wash!"

I toed the water again. It didn't feel fine.

Bash pressed his forehead against Morton's. "Whachya think, Morty-Orty-Hero-Borty-Dorty-Supergoat-Korty? You wanna bath?"

Morton pressed back. *"Maaa-haaa-haaa-haaa-haaa."*

"So into the pond we go." He tossed an arm around Morton's chocolate brown neck like they were buddies, and the two of them high-stepped into the water.

Morton hopped around, kicking waves. *"Maaa-haaa-haaa-haaa-haaa."* It was either a gleeful goat or a grumbly-goat-on-ice dance. I voted for grumpy ice cubes. But since Morton splashed deeper into the pond, I guessed he voted happy.

Bash waved a scrub brush. "C'mon, Beamer, Bonkers, and Jig. It's time to de-paint the goat."

"Or de-goat the paint." Bonkers, wearing his usual

zookeeper shorts and shirt, ran into the pond. "I've got a bucket, washcloth, and another scrub brush."

Today, Jig wore a sandy brown camouflage cap with "Ohio Farm Bureau" printed on it. He still wore his ragged red sneakers as he chased after Bash, Bonkers, and Morton. "I call the shark. I get to scrub off the shark tattoo."

"It's not a tattoo, it's a painting." I toed the water again. Still cold. "Mary Jane, how about we wait until June? Or July? I'll come back when school's out and we'll wash Morton then."

Pointy-toed boot tips tapped faster. "You painted my Morton in April. You'll clean my Morton in April. Move it."

I sucked in my breath, held it, and waded in after the guys. *Brrrrr.* It might be practically seventy degrees outside, but I was pretty sure it was minus thirty inside the pond. "Stop splashing me. It's an iceberg."

"It's great, Beamer. Hold Morton steady."

Bash, Bonkers, and Jig scrubbed. Morton rumbled a goat purr. The girls sat on the grass and hollered unhelpful things like, "You missed a spot," and "I told you that you needed shampoo."

Swirls of greens, oranges, blues, pinks, reds, purples, and yellows floated around as the dye washed off the goat of many colors.

I cupped colors into my palm, but the water whooshed between my fingers. "This can't be good for the fish. It's pollution."

Morton sighed. Bash brushed. "It's nontoxic. It's no prob."

"That's more rainbow than any trout should have."

"Could be. You know your stuff, Beams." Bonkers studied the circus colors splashing around his legs. "Told you that you'd catch the robber."

"Not me. Morton did. God protected us with a goat." A purple slosh dripped from Jig's scrub brush, drained across Morton's belly, rolled down his leg, and pooled in the pond water. I grabbed one of the scrub buckets and scooped up as much of the paint as I could. "We need to save the pond."

Bash, Bonkers, and Jig scrubbed. I skimmed temporary hair coloring, chalk dust dye, and watercolors from the pond surface. I ran ashore with each bucketful and slung the water into the grass. "Grass is a filter, right?"

Lauren popped the yellow top off a dandelion and slipped the skinny end of the hollow stem into the fat end—the first link in a dandelion chain. "Yep."

The guys scrubbed. I cleaned the water. Jag dropped bouquets of dandelions into Lauren and Mary Jane's laps. Slowly, soggily, Morton's side and back began changing from what looked like some two-year-old's coloring book to a bluish-white goat with a grayish zig-zag or two. Bash shook his scrubbing arm. "The rest will fade in a couple weeks."

Mary Jane held one end of what had grown into a twenty-foot-long dandelion chain. "Keep scrubbing."

I splish-splashed ashore with my latest bucketful of colored water. Lauren linked another looped stem. Jag ran back from across the field, cradling more dandelions. I lifted the bucket and took aim.

Mary Jane froze me with a laser blue stare. She limbered up a kicking leg that ended in a pointy-toed cowboy boot. "Don't. Even. Think. About it."

I gulped. Turned. Stumbled fifteen fast steps away from the girls. And tossed the water. *Phew.* That was a close one.

"Maaa-haaa-haaa-haaa-haaa." Morton shook himself like a dog coming in from the rain. Pond water sprayed everywhere, drenching the parts of us that weren't already soaked.

"It's a goat-powered shower!" Jig yelled. He splashed more water at Morton so Morton could spray it back.

Morton shook his head. Brown ears flapped against his face. He darted from the pond, scampered up the bank, and rolled in the grass. Goats don't own towels.

Bash threw his scrub brush like a baton. "He's done."

Mary Jane inspected the almost-white-again goat now prancing around her. "Only because he says he is. You may shampoo Morton on Monday."

Bash groaned. "Thanks loads, Mother-May-I."

Mary Jane kissed Morton's nose. "How's my good boy? Feeling all better now that that yucky graffiti is gone, aren't you? That's my good boy."

Bash and Bonkers rolled their eyes. Jig clamped his hands over his mouth to stop a chuckle.

Lauren looped the dandelion chain over Morton's horns, head, neck, and back. "It's the Goat King wearing his crown."

Goat King Morton scratched his side with a hind leg, sniffed at the royal crown links, and took a bite. He chewed and slurped the dandelion chain like a long strand of spaghetti. Lauren, Jig, and Mary Jane grabbed pieces of dandelion chain off the goat almost as fast as the goat slurped and chomped the stems. "Bad Morton. Bad Morton. Stop eating Mommy's, Aunt Lauren's, and Aunt Jecolia's crown. "

I looked at Bash. "Mommy?"

Bash looked at Bonkers. "Aunt Lauren?"

Bonkers looked at Jig. "If your sister is Aunt Jecolia, does that make you Uncle Jehoshaphat?"

"To a goat? No way!" Jig grimaced. "I'm already brother to a possum girl."

"I'll show you a possum girl." Jag charged into the water after her twin.

Jig wallowed deeper into the pond and ducked under water. His camouflage cap floated to the surface. Jag dived under after him, oversized purple gym shorts and red sneakers the last things above water before she disappeared. After a few seconds, two flame-colored heads of splaying hair bobbed just above the surface, darting and zipping at each other like a couple of drenched orange kittens.

Jig popped to the surface, followed by Jag, both of them squealing. "She tickled me!"

"Now I'm an otter girl!"

I watched the sopping twins shiver their way to shore. Mary Jane sat out of the splash zone, Morton sunning himself across her lap. Lauren rolled over. "Look at Morton. Now that he's nearly dry, his belly looks almost white again."

Bash scratched his ear. "Too bad Lake Erie is still too cold. We could take Morton to the Sunday school picnic tomorrow, and let everybody wash him."

I petted hero goat Morton's wiry, unpainted hair. "God sure answers prayers in funny ways, doesn't He?"

Bash grinned. "He likes to give us surprises."

I stretched out in the grass. At least the surprises were over this week. Weren't they?

I sat up. "What picnic?"

Chapter 22

A Dunk in the Lake

I awoke three minutes before Bash's jungle alarm screamed, whooped, trumpeted, roared, or chattered. I rolled out of bed, avoiding my slippers for fear of what might be in them.

I scratched my ribs, but quit when I figured I might look like a monkey in pajamas. I yawned, turned on the desk lamp, turned off the alarm clock, and peeked into the tadpole tank.

A miniature frog stared back at me from a leaf floating on the water.

I kicked Bash's bed. "Basher, wake up."

Bash sprung up like a Pop-Tart. "Whoa, Beamer, you're awake. What's wrong? Fire?"

"Frog." I pointed to the tank.

Bash vaulted from bed and landed beside me. "Cool. A new creature."

"Transformed. Like the caterpillars that become butterflies."

"Or moths."

"Or moths." I studied the other pollywogs in the tank. They all had front and back legs now and looked froggish. Some swished about the water with back legs and tail stubs. Some looked like froglets. And now we had one frog.

"There's another. An' another." Bash pressed his nose to the tank. "Hiya, Jamison Jumpin' Juniper Froggenfrogger."

I nudged him aside. "Don't scare him. And how come you get to name him. Hey, how do you know it's a him?"

Bash flicked water in my face. "He looks like a Jamison Jumpin' Juniper Froggenfrogger, doesn't he? And that one's Lou-Lou-Lillypad Leaperberger."

"You sound like Mary Jane talking to Morton." I fumbled into my barn clothes. "Why does morning come so early?"

Bash sorted through a heap of T-shirts on the floor and pulled one from the bottom. "'Cause if morning came at noon, it would be mor-noon." Bash frog-hopped into his jeans. "Now hurry up. The picnic's at mor-noon." And he was gone.

I sat at the desk chair to tie my shoes. "So, little frog, what's it like to transform?" The frog stared back with tiny bug eyes. I tightened the knots. "Must be cool for you to have arms and legs now. And be able to get around on land too."

The tiny frog blinked. I reached for the light. "Yeah, I agree. It's way too early to be up." I shuffled toward the stairs.

We carried pies—without chicken feathers, this time—to the dessert table under a pavilion at the top of a bluff overlooking Lake Erie. Waves whooshed to the beach in gentle splashes.

Aunt Tillie and other people from the church set covered dishes, crockpots, pans, and bowls on one of the other tables. Scents of meatloaf, ham, green beans, and more casseroles than I cared to count tickled my nose. My stomach growled.

Uncle Rollie slung a couple big jugs onto one table.

"Coffee?" someone asked.

Uncle Rollie winked at me. "Nope. Chocolate milk. I seem to have an abundance of it. Thought the kids would just love some chocolate milk with their potato salad and macaroni."

This time, I growled. I flopped onto one of the cold aluminum picnic table benches as far away from the chocolate milk as I could. Bash, Jig, Bonkers, Timmy Wayne, Billy Loomis, Kenny Mathews, and some of the other kids scampered back and forth in the grass across the edge of the bluff, searching for big ore-carrier boats on the horizon. I tried to get comfortable against the picnic table and stared out at the water. Lake Erie met the sky to the north. It stretched as far east and as far west as I could see. But Lake Erie wasn't the Atlantic Ocean. Smaller waves, if you could call those little things waves. No refreshing saltiness on the breezes. And I knew there were no dolphins.

Lauren scooted down beside me. "Your mom and dad just got here. I guess you're going home after the picnic."

"It's not home. It's the house we moved into seven months ago. It's not Virginia Beach."

"Yeah, the lake does that to me too. Makes me think of the Gulf of Mexico." Lauren's chin sunk to her chest. "I miss Florida."

I watched a wimpy wave roll onto the beach. "Lauren, don't you sometimes feel like we don't belong?"

Lauren giggled. "That's what the Farmin' and Fishin' Book says. We don't belong here. Our big brother Jesus went to heaven to make a home for us. Until then, we're supposed to enjoy the adventures He lets us have here."

"You've been reading your Bible then?"

"Sure. Haven't you?"

"Uh-huh. I found some more stuff on baptism too. After John baptized Jesus, God spoke."

Lauren nodded. "Did you memorize it?"

I scrunched my eyes closed, trying to see Matthew 3:16–17. I think I got most of it. "'He saw the Spirit of God descending like a dove and coming down on Him. And there was a voice from heaven: This is My beloved Son. I take delight in Him!'"

Someone cut loose with a shrill baseball park whistle. Half the talking stopped. Pastor Randy, a big guy with a little beard, bellowed above the other half in his preacher's voice. "Thank you all for coming out to our Sunday school picnic. Looks like we've got way too much food for just us, so don't be afraid to invite folks up from the playground and beach to help us out."

Uncle Rollie waved his baseball cap. "And chocolate milk. Don't forget the chocolate milk."

Lauren shuddered. "I never thought just plain old water would sound so good."

"And chocolate milk." Pastor Randy picked up a Bible. "Before we ask the blessing, chow down, and get out the bats and softballs, I'd like to have a short devotional. Let's gather in. Plenty of seats open."

Bash, Jig and Jag, Mary Jane, Tyler, Bonkers, and some of the rest of the kids crowded in with Lauren and me. Bonkers tossed his cap onto the table. "I hope this doesn't take long. I saw some of Mr. Burt's green bean casserole with the cheddar-flavored fried onions up there. Yum."

Bash rubbed his belly. "I just want Mrs. Patti's bread pudding. That stuff's the best."

Mary Jane waved her arms. "Shh. Pastor Randy is trying to speak."

The pastor stood at the front of the pavilion by the food. "I know you want to dig in, so we'll keep this short."

"Ha. Preachers can't say anything short!" someone hooted.

Pretty much everyone laughed, including Pastor Randy. "Keep it up and I'll show you some first-class yammering, and you'll never get to the food."

More laughing. They all seemed to be enjoying themselves. Except me.

Pastor Randy flipped open his Bible. "I'd like to talk to you a moment about—"

I shot up off the picnic bench. "What's baptism mean?"

I stood there, trembling in the silence. *Why did I do that?* Why couldn't I just think about deviled eggs and macaroni salad like the rest of the kids?

Pastor Randy smiled. "Well, that's not what I was going to talk about. But why not? Let's talk about it. Does anyone want to answer young Raymond's question?"

Bash scrambled to his feet on top of the bench seat. "It's when you throw people in th' water after they get saved. It's a splashdown celebration."

Aunt Tillie's eye ticked just before she planted her whole face in her palms. Pastor Randy's beard bobbed. "Okay, but why?"

"That's what I want to know," I mumbled and sat down. How could I be such a doofus?

Mr. Tweed raised his hand. "It's when God washes away our sins."

Pastor Randy shook his head. "Not exactly." He flipped pages in his Bible. "Here's what it says in 1 John 1:7: 'But if we walk in the light as He Himself is in the light, we have fellowship with one another, and the blood of Jesus His Son cleanses us from all sin.'"

Pastor Randy's eyes scanned us. "God let His own Son Jesus die on a cross to take the punishment for our sins. It's His blood that washes us clean." He flipped pages. "The prophet Isaiah writes in verse eighteen of the first chapter of his book, 'Come, let us discuss this,' says the LORD. 'Though your sins are like scarlet, they will be as white as snow; though they are as red as crimson, they will be like wool.'"

Pastor Randy closed his Bible. "So if it's the blood of Jesus, God's only Son, that washes us clean, what's baptism for?"

"If he doesn't know, how are we supposed to find out?" I muttered.

Lauren tapped her lip. *"Shh."*

"The answer, as always," Pastor Randy said, holding up his Bible, "can be found in here. All throughout God's Word are stories of washings. Way back in the days of Moses, he sprinkled water on the priests as a part of a purification ceremony. It didn't make them clean. It was a sign that they prepared their hearts to worship God.

"And look at this one in the sixth chapter of Romans." Pastor Randy turned the page. A couple people at the picnic tables dug out Bibles from somewhere and fluttered through the pages. "Here we go, starting with verse three.

"'Are you unaware that all of us who were baptized into Christ Jesus were baptized into His death? Therefore we were buried with Him by baptism into death, in order that, just as Christ was raised from the dead by the glory of the Father, so we too may walk in a new way of life. For if we have been joined with Him in the likeness of His death, we will certainly also be in the likeness of His resurrection.'"

Pastor Randy closed the Bible. "So what does that tell you?"

I stared at my sneakers. Bash jumped up again. "Bein' baptized is like gettin' buried in water."

"Right." Pastor Randy pointed at Bash with his Bible. "Baptism is a pledge. We are remembering what Jesus did. We go under the surface, like being buried. We are raised back out of the water, like Jesus rose from the dead to new life."

Bash waved his hand. "Like a tadpole comin' out of the water as a new creature. A frog."

Pastor Randy scratched his little beard. "Um, I don't think I get that."

I did. I pushed myself to my feet. "I want to be baptized."

The pastor smiled. "That's wonderful, Raymond. See me after the picnic, and we'll get some classes set up, schedule a date, and see what we can do."

I stretched up onto my tiptoes and waved my hand. "What about now?"

"This is a picnic, Raymond, not a church service."

I felt the eyes of a whole group of people drilling into me, a kid standing up, asking the pastor questions. My face grew hot. A Sunday school kid I didn't know snickered. My legs quivered as I dropped my eyes and started to sit.

Lauren jumped up. "Me too. I love Jesus, and I want to be baptized."

"Lauren, your new top," Mrs. Rodriguez yelped from somewhere behind us.

"It's wash-and-wear, Mom. It'll handle water. Me too."

She grabbed my hand to keep me from sitting down. Weird. I always figured girls' hands to be cold, and kind of scaly, like a lizard or something. Hers was . . . soft. Warm. Nice. I squeezed back, feeling braver.

Pastor Randy coughed. "Well, you know—"

A lawn chair creaked behind us. "Pastor, I don't know how come, but I've never been baptized either. Count me in."

I heard a rustle of clothing. Then a woman sniffled. "Pastor, I only came today for the free picnic. I've never given my heart to Jesus. I'm a good person and didn't think I needed to bother Him. But I watched the water, I heard the kids talk . . ." She blew her nose on a napkin. "Good won't get me to heaven. Only Jesus can do that. I . . . I asked Him to forgive me and save me. He did." She wiped her nose. "I'm not holding back anymore, pastor. I want to be baptized."

Pastor Randy tugged at his collar. "This isn't normally how it's done."

Bash sprang off the picnic bench. "Hey, pastor, read those verses from a couple Sundays ago. 'Member? The one in Acts when Paul and Silas were in prison, an' there was an earthquake, an' all their chains fell off, an' the jailer thought everybody got away, an' the jailer was gonna kill himself, but Paul yells, 'We're all here,' an'—"

Pastor Randy held up his hand. "Whoa, Sebastian. I remember the story. Let me turn to Acts sixteen, starting with verse thirty."

He flipped pages in his Bible. "'Then he escorted them out and said, "Sirs, what must I do to be saved?" So they said, "Believe on the Lord Jesus, and you will be saved—you and your household." Then they spoke the message of the Lord to him along with everyone in the house. He took them the same hour of the night and washed their wounds. Right away he and all his family were baptized. He brought them into his house, set a meal before them, and rejoiced because he had believed God with his entire household.'"

Bash broke in: "See. It says right away. Right away they were baptized. *Then* they ate their picnic."

Lauren raised her other hand. "What about Philip with the guy in the chariot. I just read about him in the book of Acts. The guy in the chariot yelled out, 'Look, there's water! What would keep me from being baptized?' So the guy put the brakes on the chariot and jumped in the lake so Philip could baptize him."

Pastor Randy chuckled, sat on a picnic table bench, and untied his shoe laces. "Sometimes, there's just not enough kid in us adults." He pulled off his shoes and socks, stood, pulled everything out of his pants pockets, and stuffed it into his shoes. "I'm going to need a couple elders who aren't afraid of getting wet. Grab some of those tablecloths for towels. We're going down the hill to the lake."

The pastor rolled up his pant legs. People cheered. Not your football game cheers or anything like that. They giggled and clapped and yelled, "Praise God" and "Thank You, Lord."

I was going to be baptized as a believer.

I smiled at Lauren. "Thanks. I almost sat down and died of embarrassment."

She grinned back. "No prob. It's what friends do. And Ray?"

"Yeah?"

"Could you stop squeezing my hand now? It kinda hurts."

Yipes. I was still holding a girl's hand. I practically flung it away. My cheeks started burning all over again. Lauren giggled. "You're cute when you're embarrassed. Better hurry or you'll miss your own baptism." She spun on her toes and bolted for the stairs leading down to the beach.

Chapter 23

The Great Frog Escape

Back at the farm, I hugged Mom and Dad. "I'm glad you got to be at the baptism."

"You don't give a guy much notice," Dad said. "I didn't have a chance to change into my baptism suit."

Mom grinned. "You don't have a baptism suit."

"Well, if I did, I wouldn't have had time to change into it. The kid likes to spring surprises."

Aunt Tillie's eye twitched. "Please, no more surprises. I believe we've had enough for one week."

Dad sniffed at a leftover Oreo cookie from the April Fool's package, wrinkled his nose, and put it back. "The kids catching the robber was an awfully big surprise."

Mom bit her lip. "I'm proud of you, Raymond, but honestly, I wish you had run away."

"That was my plan, Mom."

Bash pumped his fist. "You shoulda seen Ray-Ray Sunbeam Beamer."

"Stop calling me that."

"I think it's cute," Mom said. "You are my Merry Little Sunshine, you know."

I slapped my forehead. "*Moo-oooommmm!* Don't give the doofus any ideas."

"You shoulda seen the Merry Little Sunshine. He played the best prank of all this week."

I shook my head. "It wasn't a prank. I didn't want him to shoot anybody."

"Squirt, you mean."

"Whatever. I told him the money was in the stump. It was."

Bash grinned. "And?"

I couldn't help it. I grinned too. "And Morton was just waiting for someone to play with."

"Smart, cousin. Smart."

"Only because you were crazy enough to teach a goat to head butt."

"Goats already know that game. You were the one who said we should paint 'im."

"I never said that."

Bash punched my shoulder. "You're pretty cool, cousin."

"I am? Thanks."

Mom shivered. "I still wish you hadn't faced the robber. You could have been hurt."

"We prayed. God answered prayer. Just not the way I wanted Him to."

Bash ran around the table. "God always answers better than we know how. He's the best Surpriser of all."

I poked at my glasses. "So what's going to happen to the robber?"

"He'll be in the county jail until the trial. I suspect he'll be going to prison for a while." Uncle Rollie shook his head. "I hate to see anyone go to prison. Such a waste of what God could have done with a person."

"So why'd he do it?"

Uncle Rollie stirred some chocolate milk into his coffee. "He's not much more than a kid, really. He got fed up having to follow rules and figured he could make a better life if he ran away and did what he wanted. It never seems to work out that way."

Uncle Rollie sipped from his mug and smiled. "Best-tasting coffee creamer we ever had. Anyway, the kid told Deputy Timothy he was tired and wanted to go home, but didn't have any money. He didn't know how to get any. I guess he didn't think about how several of us could use help at planting season. Instead, he was trying to steal enough money for gas and food to get back to Phoenix. Except we don't keep a lot of money lying around."

"You're going to visit him, aren't you, Pops?"

"Sure thing, champ. He's scared. He needs a friend. I can introduce him to the best Friend a person can have." He tugged at his mustache. "I wonder if we can do a baptism in the county jail."

Dad looked at his watch. "We better get a move on. We need to get home. There's church in the morning, and then it's back to school on Monday for Ray."

Uncle Rollie stood. "Just a minute, Frankie-Frankie-Frankenstein. We have a little parting gift for you."

Uncle Rollie opened the refrigerator and pulled out a gallon of chocolate milk. And another. And another. He reached in again for two more. And yet another. "Six gallons is a good start. I have four or five more gallons for you in the basement refrigerator."

My stomach did a backflip. I gagged. If there'd been a mirror, mirror on the kitchen wall, it probably would've shown me as the greenest one of all.

Uncle Rollie chuckled. "Make sure the boy drinks a gallon or so with every meal. He earned it."

Mom opened her mouth to say something—"He's not allowed to drink chocolate milk" is what I hoped to hear—but she closed it and shook her head. She ruffled my hair. "Raymond, I think you should go pack up your things."

Oh, great. Now the grown-ups would be able to talk. I figured I knew what about. And I'd be drinking more chocolate milk. Yippee.

Bash headed for the stairs. "C'mon, Merry Little Sunshine. I'll help."

"Stop calling me that. Mom, did you have to call me that in front of the Basher?"

It didn't take long to round up my clothes and cram them into the backpack. I strained my ears trying to figure out if there was any yelling going on downstairs. It sounded more like snickers and chuckles, but I couldn't be sure.

"I'd like to come back for the summer, but I'm probably going to be grounded until I'm forty-seven. We'll be too old to have fun then."

"I'm already working on plans for April Fool's Day next year. What a great holiday! Maybe the chickens can lay fried eggs. Or if April Fool's isn't over spring break next year, I'm gonna dress up Gulliver J. McFrederick the Third in my clothes, take him to school, and enroll him as a new student. Mrs. Cranberry will have a cow when she sees a pig in a front row desk. It'll be great."

I shook my head.

Bash picked up the basketball. "So what was it like?"

"What?"

"The baptism." He stretched in the middle of the floor and tossed the basketball toward the overhead light.

"You better not miss. I mean, you better miss."

The ball came within a half inch of the light, then fell softly into Bash's hands just above his nose. "Easy. It's a piece of strawberry-rhubarb pie." He spun the ball at the light again. "So what was it like?"

I snatched the ball out of the air. If he broke the light, we'd both be in for it. "It was cold. But nice."

Bash found his rolled-up dirty socks and pitched them toward the light. "Did you gag?"

I sat on my bed and spun the basketball. "No. Pastor Randy held one side and Mr. Gobnotter had my other shoulder. Pastor Randy told me to plug my nose. Then they lowered me backward into the water."

209

Bash caught the sock roll. I hugged the basketball to my chest. "I started to panic a little. It's really weird to go over backward in water like that."

Bash flung the socks at the ceiling light again. "Then what?"

"They pulled me up out of the water. And I stood there, gulping air. I could breathe."

Bash caught the socks near his nose and grimaced. "Yuck. So'd you hear any voices?"

I bounced the basketball between my hands. "Not really. No doves or voices booming, 'This is my son and I delight in him.'" I leaned forward until my chin rested on the ball. "But I heard it inside. Not a real voice. Just something inside, where I feel Jesus every day. He liked it. I've been through the water with God."

"Yeah. It was like that for me too." Bash sat up. "You know the Farmin' and Fishin' Book says we gotta be baptized with fire too."

I froze. "Fire? For real?"

"When John the Baptist was baptizing all those people, he told them, 'I baptize you with water, but One is coming who is more powerful than I.'" Bash squeezed his eyes shut. "Oh yeah, he said, 'He will baptize you with the Holy Spirit and fire.'"

"Whoa. I don't want to burn down the chicken coop again like last winter."

"Not real fire. He's talkin' inside fire. When you let God's Spirit take over everything in your life, it's like being on fire for God." Bash threw the socks underhand at the ceiling light. "Blood, water, an' fire. It's in the book."

"The Farmin' and Fishin' Book?"

"Of course."

I set the basketball beside me. "Being a Christian is confusing. There's too much to know."

"Nope. It's simple. All you gotta do is read the Farmin' and Fishin' Book and talk with God. He likes that. He talks to you all day long inside."

"Where the fire is?"

"Where you let His Son in. Now God's Spirit can show you everything to do. Father, Son, and Spirit."

I shook my head. I was going to have to do a lot more talking with God. But that was okay. I'd asked God to forgive all the bad stuff in me, and He did. I let Jesus into my heart, and He filled that empty thing inside me. Now I was letting God change me from His blobby pollywog into the really cool frog He wants me to be. Change can be hard and scary. But God's adventures always work out right even when I have no clue what's going on.

I looked around the room for any of my stuff I forgot to pack. "God sure likes surprises, doesn't He?" I wandered over to Bash's desk and peeked inside the fish tank. "Bye, little pollywogs."

Little blobs with legs and tiny tails darted through the water. I looked harder. Only little blobs. And not enough of them.

"Say, Bash, what happened to the tadpoles that already transformed to baby frogs?"

Bash studied the tank. He dropped to his knees and looked under the beds. "I don't know. Did the praying mantis come back?"

I looked under pillows and dirty socks. "No. We closed the window."

Bash burrowed through his Legos. "Jamison Jumpin' Juniper Froggenfrogger. Lou-Lou-Lillypad Leaperberger. Where are you?"

Bash chewed on his tongue. "I don't get it, Beamer. They couldn't just disappear."

"Then where are they?"

A shrill scream made us both jump.

"What was that?"

"It sounded like it came from the bathroom."

The scream cut the air again. But this time it sounded like, *"Se-bassssshhhhhh-tiannnnnnnnnnnnnn!"*

"How about that," Bash said. "Ma found the frogs."

I grabbed my backpack and bolted for the door.

Acknowledgments

Once again, I owe a huge Play-Doh party to my critique group, the kids of American Christian Fiction Writers Clubhouse 206: Debbie Archer, Kate Hinke, Leigh DeLozier, Dawn Overman, Cynthia Toney, and Michelle Kaderly Welsh. They are great "critters," encouragers, and terrific authors as well. I eagerly anticipate having all of their books on my shelves.

I send super thanks to "Jay," who provided my Fortress of Writing Solitude when deadlines threatened to roll me over.

Much gratitude goes to marvel editor Jamie Chavez for clipping and clapping, and to publisher Dan Lynch at B&H Kids for turning the kids loose to romp through this pasture again.

Lots of love—and flowers would be nice—for my personal copy editor, Terry Heidrich Cole, who didn't know that "I do" included punctuating lots of literary pigs, chickens, and cows.

And, as always, praise God, from whom all blessings flow, including the blessing of laughter.